STORMING AREA 51: HORROR AT THE GATE

MICHELLE RIVER   BEN HARE

ALANNA ROBERTSON-WEBB   DREW STARLING

ZANE HENSAL

EERIE RIVER PUBLISHING

Paperback ISBN: 9781691186983

Edited by: Ben Hare and Alanna Robertson-Webb
Formatting by: Michele Freeman
Cover designed by: Michelle River

AUTHOR NOTES

This book was created and collaboratively written by five unique indie authors. Michelle River, Ben Hare, Alanna Robertson-Webb, Drew Starling and Zane Hensal.

We challenged ourselves to write and tell a story through the voices and points of view of different characters. The story is based around a five day period leading up to the Facebook event "Storm Area 51", and the characters themselves weave us a tale of sinister plots, alien threats, government conspiracies and rescue missions along the way.

We hope you enjoy it as much as we did.

CONTENTS

PART 1
ELAIN   3

PART 2
CARRIE   17
ELAIN   24
NATE   33
NEILA   43
ELAIN   50

PART 3
GERALD   57
ELAIN   68
CARRIE   78
NEILA   88
RANDY   94

PART 4
GERALD   107
RANDY   119
CARRIE   126

PART 5
LOGAN   135

PART 6
GERALD   151

ELAIN   161
NEILA   174
CARRIE   180
GERALD   189
RANDY   200

EPILOGUE
September 21, 2019   209

ABOUT THE AUTHORS
Michelle River   217
Alanna Robertson-Webb   219
Ben Hare   221
Drew Starling   223
Zane Hensal   225

PART 1

SEPTEMBER 15, 2019

S till no signal.

I checked my phone for the umpteenth time in the last five minutes, and it was still the same. No bars, no reception, no nothing. We were officially in a dead zone.

"Will you put your phone away?" Greg said. He was running up to me from the water, and I could feel the cool drops hit me as he sat down with a *humph* next to me. Trevor, our four year old son, bounded behind him and threw himself at me in a giant, wet hug. He giggled and ran off, heading towards the wagon of toys. He immediately went for his spade and shovel, and began to play in the sand.

I smiled and watched him play, clutching my

phone to my chest for a moment before relenting and putting it away when Greg made another noise. He knew what I was doing, and how hard it was waiting for an email from the doctor's office. My test results were supposed to be coming back this week, which was the exact reason why I needed this vacation.

The last few months since finding the small tumour were rough. The course of radiation, and the months of medications like methotrexate, had done a number on me physically and emotionally. I was exhausted, and it didn't help that I was keeping everything secret from my parents, who were here with us. I didn't want to worry them, and I planned on telling them once I got the all-clear, which I was hoping would come in the form of an email any day.

As I watched my parents frolicking in the water with my nephews, Thomas and Adrien, and my sister Ashley, I admitted to myself that this was a little bit relaxing. I eased down into the chair, the tension almost letting me unclench my shoulders. The large, sandy beach was free of debris, and it was big enough to set our travelling circus of beach tents, umbrellas and wagon of toys on. It was also completely private. The lake itself was beautiful and clean, perfectly circular in shape, with soft sand and a gentle slope into the water's edge.

"Get in that water Elain, it's beautiful," I heard Greg say. "I have Trevor, you go and cool off. It's too warm, and you look really uncomfortable."

He wasn't wrong, I *was* really uncomfortable. No matter what I did, I couldn't shake the nagging feeling that something bad was going to happen.

"I know, I need to let it all go," I said as I chewed on my lip. Easier said than done.

"Look, let's make a deal," he turned me to face him, his voice serious. "You go swim, enjoy the lake. Take it easy, go talk with your family, do some laps. Do *something*. Trevor's fine with me. I'll take care of him."

I watched him for a moment, a lump forming in my chest. It would be so simple to just let it go; I needed this as much as he did. He needed to know I trusted him, and I did. It was my anxiety that was causing this. I was just worried for myself, my family and for what would happen. He was right, Trevor would be fine.

"You're right. Go, go play. Just ... "

"I know, I know, don't let him eat the sand." He gave me an awkward salute and headed off towards our son, and I tried to release the tension in the pit of my stomach.

I swam the length of the small lake, letting the

months of work and life stress leach from my body into the cool depths. I looked towards the shore, watching Trevor with his much older cousins Adrien and Thomas. They began walking buckets of sand towards the line of beach chairs, my nephews' bright red hair standing out in the sun in contrast to Trevor's blond hair. He had gotten it from his father. *Must be time for sand creatures,* I thought to myself. It was our family tradition, and the boys loved it. Every beach vacation we took turns burying each other in the sand, building a mound and then transforming them into a creature made of sand. It made for great family photos, everyone's head popping out of the sand above a unique monster. The whole family loved it.

It looked like Pierce, my sister's boyfriend, was going to be the first sand victim of the day. He had barely had time to get himself positioned under the umbrella before all three of them surrounded him, buckets in hand, and began covering him with a mountain of sand.

By the time I had made it out Pierce was passed out under a blanket of sand, made up to look like a mermaid, seashell bra and all. I had to give it to him, he did well with Ashley's boys. Even if he was a bit of a meathead.

Hours later, sun-baked and exhausted, we packed up our beach gear and walked back to the cabin. Pierce looked worse for wear, his eyes blood-shot and his legs straining to hold his weight like he was sleepwalking.

He had slept for a good few hours under the sand, so maybe that was why he looked so groggy? Or maybe the water I saw him chugging before his nap was a bit more than water; that wouldn't surprise me. It wouldn't be the first time one of us had gotten drunk the first night in, but I hadn't seen any booze in the cooler, I wondered how he snuck some down without us noticing.

I saw him stumble on the last step as he headed inside the cottage, and I was shocked to see red, swollen dots littering the soles of his feet and palms of his hands like little insect bites. Not only was he drunk, but the poor fool was covered in bug bites. I shook my head as I watched him excuse himself to the bedroom, presumably to sleep off his stupor, and we continued on with our day.

I had just shut the bedroom door after tucking Trevor in for the night when I saw Pierce next.

"Feeling any better?" I asked, looking him over. His hands were tucked into his cargo shorts, and I wondered if they were still as red and swollen as they were earlier. He gave me a strange look, his eyes wide and his smile overly large. I could see every tooth in his mouth, a stark contrast to the gruff, half-nod I normally received from him in passing. "Yes, everything is perfect." He licked his teeth, his eyes roaming down the hallway to see if anyone was around. He was starting to give me the creeps. "Would you mind coming..."

"Elain, honey. We're going for a dip in the hot tub. Are you coming?" Greg called to me, unaware of the unusual scene he had just interrupted. I quickly walked towards him, leaving Pierce alone in the darkened hallway.

"Just go," I said under my breath to Greg as I shooed him down the hall to our bedroom.

"What was that about?"

"I don't know, but he was giving me the creeps. Let's just get in the hot tub and relax."

Mom, Dad and my brother William were already neck-deep in the whirling water by the time

Greg and I had gotten changed into our suits and made it outside. Ashley was still in the kitchen piling beers into the cooler so that they'd be cold when we needed them. It didn't matter how hot it was outside, we were not a family that could turn down the opportunity to drink beer in a hot tub.

"That's the good stuff," I said as I dipped my toes into the water, slowly sinking into the steamy bath, jets on high. "What an amazing place, Will. How the heck did you find this so fast?"

"You wouldn't believe me, but a guy from work practically begged me to stay here," he said as he dunked his head under the water quickly, then coming up and reaching for a beer. "He overheard me mention how our last place fell through and he said he had the perfect spot. Voila. Here we are."

"It is perfect William, you did a great job finding this place," Mom said, her small hands coming out to pat him on the shoulder. *Always her little baby*, I thought as I tried not to roll my eyes.

"I would definitely come here again," Dad chimed in. His eyes were closed, and his head was relaxed back against the cushion. "Perfect spot, even the lake. Nice and clean. Must be all those zebra mussels filtering the water clean."

I stifled a laugh and exchanged a knowing look

with Greg. It was a running joke in my family anytime Dad came upon clean water he exclaimed it was from the zebra mussels that big ships brought in. I didn't feel like going into the details of how that would be impossible for a lake like this, so we all stayed silent and let him float in peace, content to dream about zebra mussels cleaning the great lakes of Ontario.

"Hey Pierce, you coming in?" It wasn't until Greg called out from beside me that I noticed Pierce had crept outside. He was watching us silently from the shadow of the doorway, but he didn't look right. Sweat had begun to form on his brow, and his body was vibrating. His head was shaking a 'no' at the site of the tub. Thomas, who was sitting on a patio chair before this, came up behind Pierce. He motioned for us to be quiet with his finger, then he grabbed a hold of Pierce, pushing him towards the hot tub.

"Come on Pierce, get in," Thomas joked, edging him closer.

Pierce yelled, digging his heels into the ground. He whipped his body around and threw his arms around Thomas, locking him into a headlock and dragging him back towards the house. Thomas struggled, and both of them fell violently on the hard deck.

My mother's screams sliced the air as William and Greg both jumped from the tub, forcefully separating Pierce and Thomas to opposite sides of the patio before things escalated even further. Greg stood silently over Pierce, and we all glared at my sister's boyfriend. Pierce's breath was heavy as he tried to regain control, and there was spittle dripping out of the corner of his mouth with each exhale. His eyes were wide, and the red welts on his hands looked angry as he brushed the sweat from his brow.

The door swung open and Ashley immediately ran toward Thomas, making sure he wasn't hurt. He shook off her probing, motherly hand and stood up, trying to look like he didn't care, but he only succeeded in looking young and betrayed.

"What the fuck, man!?" Thomas yelled.

"I'm ... I'm ... sorry," Pierce stammered. His breath was still ragged, but was now under control. "I'm so sorry Thomas, I just reacted. It wasn't about you. I just, I just really didn't want to get pushed in. I don't like hot water."

"You thought it was okay to lay hands on my son because you didn't want to get wet? What the fuck, Pierce?" Ashley stood in front of him, hands on her hips, toe tapping a manic rhythm. Pierce's pleading eyes stared back at her from where Greg had dragged him.

"Absolutely not." He looked directly at Thomas this time. "I'm very sorry, Thomas. I think I'm just overheated. It was a really long day, and I think I got heat stroke or something. I just don't feel like myself."

"It's okay," Thomas said quietly, still unsure of what had just happened. He wasn't the only one.

"No, it isn't. I'm going to go inside and sleep on the couch in the basement. It is cooler down there, and I don't want to make anyone uncomfortable."

Too late for that.

Greg stepped back, allowing Pierce to stand up without bumping into him. He sheepishly looked at Ashley, who stepped away from his now-outstretched arm, and she walked towards the hot tub without another word.

We were quiet, most of us shell-shocked by what had just happened. The only sound was the whirling water of the hot tub, and our collective breathing.

"Seriously guys, can someone hand me a beer please?" Ashley said as she stripped down to her bathing suit and crawled in. "I don't want to talk about it, just get back in the tub and let's try to have a good night. I'll deal with him in the morning."

I didn't know what to say. You could cut the tension with a knife, but there was something else going on, something that I just couldn't put my finger on. It bothered me, deeply. I eased back into the tub, grabbing Greg's hand as he crawled back in next me. I leaned over, giving him a kiss on the cheek, and whispered, "We're locking the bedroom doors tonight. Something is off with Pierce. I don't trust him."

PART 2

SEPTEMBER 16, 2019

CARRIE

6:20 A.M.

The airport smelled of recycled air, sweat, and burnt coffee.

So this is what all the Vegas hoopla is about, I thought as I trudged through the mass of sleepy bodies headed towards the conveyor belt. The morons were probably about to have another hour-long wait for their luggage.

You wouldn't catch me standing around waiting for hours for someone else to fetch my bag, like some lazy idiot. Knowing my luck it would have made its way into some baggage handler's car halfway across the country by now.

You just can't trust people, plain and simple.

"Excuse me, ma'am," I heard someone say as he shoved their way past me, making a beeline towards the bathroom. I cringed at the physical intrusion of personal space, and I bit my lip to stifle my first reaction of sticking my foot out and tripping him on the way over. My body was on full alert my stress level from the long flights were starting to make me mean.

One... two... three... four... five... I started counting to ten in my head, a sure sign I was upset. I had been doing it since I could remember, something my first therapist told me to do years ago to help calm my nerves and bring me back to reality. I mainly used it in crowds, or when I felt anxious. It seemed like I had counted to ten a thousand times over the three long flights it took to get from Nome to Vegas.

I only had a few memories of my childhood, of a time before anxiety had become a leading factor in my everyday life. Before the Grey Aliens had abducted me from our hunting cabin in the woods when I was five and used me for their disgusting experiments. I used to smile, to laugh and play with the other kids, but then everything changed.

They had found me in the woods after four days of torture, welts and marks all over my body. The doctors told my parents that I had been abused, probably by a vagrant passing through. They said I was lucky to be alive, but I wasn't lucky. It wasn't luck that I survived, and it wasn't a human that had done

this to me. It was them. The Greys. I clearly remembered their large, black eyes. Their smooth, cold, grey
skin. The poking and prodding, the scratching and
taking.

For years doctors and therapists, one after the
other, told me it was a false memory. I knew the truth
though, and so did they. Aliens had done this to me,
and I wasn't going to let the Government cover it
all up.

I checked my watch: only 6:25 a.m. local time. I
had left Nome, Alaska last night at 7:45 p.m., and
between the flight from Anchorage that left at 9:55
p.m. to Seattle, then the overnight stay on the hard
airport floor, waiting for the flight to McCarran in
Las Vegas this morning. I don't think I slept more
than 3 hours combined. I was exhausted.

I could hear my stomach demanding sustenance
but I ignored it, eager to get out of the airport and on
the road as fast as possible. Like my partner Patricia
had suggested, multiple timed before I left, I made
sure to call a taxi once the plane hit the tarmac so
that it would be waiting for me by the time I made it
through the airport.

"You don't want to have to wait hours for a ride,"
I remembered Patricia saying as she had run through
the packing checklist for the fourth time. I imagined

she was envisioning throngs of people running towards the exits, all needing rides away from the airport en masse. She always worried excessively, but I found it endearing how she needed to plan every detail of every day.

"Don't worry babe, everything will be fine, just like we talked about." I chuckled as I wrapped her in a warm hug.

"I do worry, that's what I do," she said, and it was true.

I had met Patricia thirteen years before, when I was twenty-five years old, at an Alien Abduction support group of all places. Unbeknown to me at the time, the adorable lady in her mid-thirties holding the meetings and offering support, as well as jam-filled cookies, would become my girlfriend and eventually life partner. We connected over our past traumas of being abducted as children, and we bonded over the jeers and taunts our fellow peers and family members would hurl behind our backs and at our faces. We cried in each other's arms as we recounted the years of abuse and feeling like we were crazy, thankful that we had finally found one another.

Although our childhood experiences were very similar, Patricia's continuous abductions into adulthood have left her in fear of the outside world. Anything different, anything abnormal outside of our small little home, effects her. Her agoraphobia was getting worse with each passing encounter with the Greys. Turning our once quaint life into a prison.

The moment the Facebook event for Storm Area 51 had been posted, we knew I had no choice. I was going. It was a war cry for all of us believers. A call to rally together and demand answers from the Government and shed light on the conspiracy that kept so many in the dark. It was my God-given right to protest, and I was going to use it. The citizens of the world needed to know the truth, and since Patricia couldn't go, I was going for her. That led me on the road to Rachel, Nevada, and to the gates of Area 51 by myself. By myself, but not alone.

To my delight and surprise, I had found a group of like-minded individuals on Facebook who also planned to head towards the gate in protest. Together we discussed our plan of attack, masses of messages sent between us. We would head to the gates early to set up camp, infiltrate the other groups that were there for fun, and then try to show them the truth of what was really happening beyond the gates. We'd tell them our stories, and enlighten them about the horrors of the Government's conspiracy and how it had been feeding us lies our entire lives.

We had flyers, t-shirts, hats and other materials printed so that we could be a visible force in the crowd. Everything had our logo "The truth is HERE" plastered across it, and the more I read it the more I liked it. These were our uniform of truth, and we would wear them proudly as we walked around. We were spreading the word, and we were letting the Government know that know we wouldn't take it anymore.

Patricia and I had planned my trip down to the last detail. We had rented a large RV from a local dealership so that I could stay on site for the week. I pre-ordered crates of water from Costco, along with some other supplies that were scheduled to be picked up once the store was opened that morning. I just needed to get out of the godforsaken airport!

I bolted through the crowd of passengers. Their wide smiles and screams of joy as they embraced family and friends at the doors leading out of the baggage area were far too bright and loud for this early in the morning. I rolled my eyes and grunted, meeting the stare of an older gentleman that had been on the same flights as me the entire way. He returned the eye roll, and although we hadn't spoken a word the entire eleven hour and forty-five minute trip we understood each other perfectly. We both thought they were all idiots, and I almost smiled.

I checked my watch again, but it was only 6:31 a.m.. I kicked myself for not packing something to eat, then I headed towards the small airport convenience shop to see if they had any overpriced garbage I could grab to eat on the go. The camper rental dealership was only eighteen minutes from the airport, if what Google Maps told me was true, but knowing my luck my taxi driver would want to take the scenic route. I didn't have time for a real breakfast since they opened at 8:00 a.m., and I wanted to be there right on time. I had a long day ahead of me.

ELAIN

10:40 A.M.

The heat of the morning hit us the moment we walked out of the cabin, making me want to retreat back into the air conditioned walls and waste the day away inside. But Trevor wouldn't let me, and with his small hand firmly grasping mine he pulled me past the threshold and into the humidity. I was all for the last dog days of summer, but besides crazy schedules and life we normally chose September for one very big reason: it wasn't supposed to be so fucking hot.

Greg was still sleeping off the beer from last night, having had a few too many after the Pierce incident. I couldn't blame him, and had I felt any better I would have done the same.

Hand-in-hand, we made our way down the little

path where we found the rest of the family already in the water splashing about. Everyone except for Pierce, who was rummaging around our little tent city of umbrellas and chairs as he dug in the sand.

Pierce had woken up early and made a hot breakfast for everyone, and he set up our beach gear as an apology for the night before. He knew he was in the dog house, and it looked like he was doing everything he could to get out of it. I hoped Ashley knew what she was getting into, since until last night I had thought Pierce was perfect for her. He didn't require much attention, and he liked just hanging out and playing with her kids, which was a big bonus. He may not have been the sharpest nail in the bucket, but he was a pleasant human being who didn't normally offend anyone. He genuinely seemed to care for her, but after last night I wasn't so sure he was the person I thought he was. Something dark was behind those eyes, something violent.

"Hey Elain," Pierce waved up at me from from beneath one of the umbrellas. It looked like he was digging holes under them. No, not holes, more like shallow trenches. They were about half a foot deep, and long enough to fully lie down in.

"Morning Pierce, whatcha doing?"

"I'm making a place for everyone to get buried in

the sand," he said, his grin so big that I was sure his teeth would crack from the pressure. "Come lay down, you can get buried first. I had such a great sleep yesterday in the sand, so I thought it would be fun for Trevor and I to bury everyone today."

He stretched out his arm, waving me towards him. The red spots on his hand were still there, but they didn't look as red and angry. I wondered if they were sand flea bites still from yesterday? I was definitely not going to become a sand monster if those were bad this year.

"Want to be a sand creature Mommy?" Trevor let go of my hand and ran over to the sand toys, grabbing the largest bucket he could find.

"Not now monster. It is too hot today, Mommy wants to go swimming first," I said, taking Trevor by the hand and ushering him into the water.

Trevor charged towards the water, the hesitant steps of yesterday forgotten. We splashed and swam back and forth between my mom and dad, who were happy to play lifeguard. I watched as Ashley reluctantly agreed to get out of the water and play sand monster, lying in one of the trenches Pierce had already dug out while he slowly covered her. He meticulously worked at her legs first, making sure to encase them completely before moving upwards to her thighs. She smiled at him awkwardly and tried to make small talk, but he didn't notice or care. He was focused on the sand, how it mounded over her and spilled down around her.

Trevor and I had progressed to the deeper part of the lake, Trevor in his life jacket with me as the makeshift swim coach, when I noticed we were the only ones left in the water.

"Watch me Mommy!" he exclaimed as he jumped off the lone rock nearby, splashing and kicking his feet to swim towards me.

"Wow Trevor, big splashes," I said.

I glanced towards the shore, and that's when I saw them. They were all buried, every single one of my family. they were perfect little mounds, one after the other like a row of speed bumps along a sand road.

I could see Pierce hurrying back and forth between the mounds, hand-feeding sandwiches to his buried prisoners. A feeling of unease set in, and my skin began to crawl as I watched my mom take another bite of sandwich. With her body hidden under a blanket of sand she looked like a ghoulish monster.

This is wrong, something is wrong, I thought.

"You getting hungry, monster?" I asked. It

was well after noon, and the sun had already passed its peak so I knew he would be starving by now. Trevor nodded frantically, and I quickly took him on my hip and carried him out of the water.

"Hey guys, we're going to head back for lunch," I announced as we emerged from the water, the hot sand burning my feet. Trevor immediately ran towards the human sand mound that was my father, tracing his fingers in the sand like a pen on paper as he drew a flower.

To my surprise everyone seemed to be sleeping, their heads propped on folded towels, their eyes shut and mouths open slightly.

"I made a spot for you over here." I jumped at Pierce's voice from behind me. He pointed to a trench dug in the sand, his smile wide and tense. "Trevor can help me bury you. That will be fun, won't it Trevor?"

I looked between the trench and Pierce's manic smile. His eyes, wide and bloodshot, twitching with the effort to remain open as he stared at me.

Despite the heat a cold shiver ran through me, my lizard-brain instinct kicking in at the bizarre scene. It was screaming at me to run from whatever this was. I shook my head no, suddenly unsure of my

own words or thoughts, and walked towards my
father.

"Dad," I whispered, "Dad, are you okay?"

Pierce came up behind me, his body too close for
comfort. I could feel his hot leg sliding along mine,
which was still cool and damp from the water.

"Dad." Louder this time. He grunted slightly and
began to shake himself awake. His eyes slowly
opened, squinting in the brightness of the light.

"What …. What's going on?"

"Nothing Dad," I sighed in relief. For a moment
I had thought the worst had happened, and that I
was staring at my family's corpses. "We're just
heading in for lunch, did you want to join us?"

"No, no. It is quite comfortable here actually.
Great place for a nap." His smile grew wider. "You
two should join us. Pierce made sandwiches, no need
to leave the beach. It's a beach day, after all."

I shook my head at the absurdity of it all. In what
world would I think a fun day at the beach would be
getting buried in the sand and fed sandwiches while
I napped?

"I don't think so Dad. You know I hate eating at
the beach, sand gets into everything. Besides Trevor
needs a nap, a real nap in his bed. We're just going to
walk back to the cottage."

"Alright dear. See you in a little bit then," Dad replied around a yawn, his eyes closing fully with his last word.

I wanted to wake the rest of them up to make sure they were all okay, but Pierce was watching me like a hawk eyeing a mouse, so I quickly picked Trevor up and started walking to the path. Pierce followed on my heels, almost herding me like a sheep towards the trail. His invasion of my personal space made the hairs on the back of my neck stand on edge. He mirrored every step I took, like a dance I didn't know the steps to. When my feet were finally planted in the cool, soft forest floor I shifted Trevor off my hip, then turned to tell him to back off. He was already yards away though, heading back towards the group and leaving me confused and unsettled. Something was definitely off with Pierce.

The air conditioning in the cabin was comforting, but it did nothing to ease my mind. I found Greg heating up some leftover burgers, and I immediately told him how strange the whole thing at the beach had been.

"I don't know what's going on, but he's giving me the creeps," I said.

"Look, I know last night was weird, but we've known the guy for a year. This is the first time he's done or said anything strange, so maybe cut him some slack?"

"That we know of!" I exclaimed. "I'm going to get in the car and see if I can drive somewhere with internet so I can Google this guy. Something just isn't right."

"That's crazy Elain, even for you."

"I know it is, but I just have to get out of here. I'm going to obsess about this until I do." He knew I was right; I wouldn't be able to let this go until I knew for sure. It was one of the many quirks he had accepted when he married me eight years ago.

"Okay, I'll get Trevor fed and put him down for a nap. You'll have to take your parent's camper though, since they're parked behind us."

"Shit. Oh well, gotta learn how to drive one for when we turn old and grey I guess. We'll need one with a bathroom you know."

He laughed at that, and I walked towards Trevor who was sitting on the couch watching a cartoon. How he had learned how to turn on the satellite with so many remotes is beyond me, and I felt a little wave of pride as I gave him a quick kiss on the cheek.

"Okay Monster, I'm headed out for a bit and I'll be back soon. Be good for Dad. I love you."

"Love you too Mommy. Bring me back a treat, please."

After a solid half hour of driving to get decent reception, and then a quick stop to the nearest Tim Hortons for Trevor's treat, I had to admit Greg was right. I couldn't find anything untoward about Pierce; he seemed to be just a normal guy. I reluctantly made my way back home defeated with a fifty pack of Timbits, Trevor's favourite one-bite donut treat, on the passenger seat for everyone to share. Maybe my imagination was running wild and I was making a bigger deal out of it than I should.

Half an hour later I pulled into the cottage driveway, feeling exhausted and defeated from the day. I looked at the cottage, then towards the back of the camper and decided to see how comfortable the sleeping quarters really were. No one would miss me for an hour or two, and Trevor was safe with Greg. I pulled closed the cotton floral curtain Mom had made to allow for privacy in the rear of the van, and snuggled into the familiarity of my parents' scents.

"Nate, when will Mom be home?" my little sister Maya asked, juice box and Barbie in hand, her blonde hair freshly ponytailed by my grandmother.

"In a little bit. Now go play, then she'll be here before you know it," I replied as I stared at my phone, awaiting a text from Mom.

Mom had been unusually quiet since her last text last night, and unlike normal she didn't call first thing in the morning to wish us all a good day and let us know when she would be coming home. This morning it was just a quick response of "Home by six." when Grandma had reached out and texted her at Maya's request.

"You'd think they'd get tired of going to Niagara

Falls every year," said Grandma as she walked into the living room and took a seat on the couch across from me.

"You know Mom, she likes her traditions," I said, looking at the TV. "Plus there's lots of outlet stores, so all the girls get a shopping day or whatever."

The five years since Dad had passed away in a work accident had been hard on all of us, but especially Mom. The first year was the hardest I think, with her taking on all of the responsibilities of the household by herself while juggling three kids that were grieving in their own ways. After her breakdown Grandma had moved into the spare bedroom, and she started helping around the house and made Mom take a vacation.

"Now don't go crazy and leave me here with these terrors for a week, just get out for a weekend. Head up to Niagara Falls, it's nice and relaxing there. Go shopping, drink some wine, and come back home," I had overheard her say.

That was four years ago. Grandma now lived back at home in Boston, but the tradition of the weekend getaway, and Grandma's visit, lived on.

"You're lucky I like you kids. Nothing like driving all the way from Boston to Baltimore in a rainstorm."

"At least it won't be raining on your return trip," I said as I held up my phone. "My weather app says it's sunny skies tomorrow."

"Whoop-te-do," she said with a chuckle. She got up and walked into the kitchen.

"Where's Lily?" I asked, following her.

"In her room. She wants to take Maya and go to her friend's house, but I told her to wait until your mother gets home. God, the older that girl grows the sassier she gets," Grandma exclaimed. Lily was thirteen, two years younger than me.

"Yeah. She's a big pain in the butt most of the time," I said as I opened the fridge and retrieved a soda. The cool air of the fridge felt nice, especially since Grandma insisted on turning the air conditioner off when she arrived on Friday night. "Nobody needs air conditioning in September, just open a window to let the breeze in," she'd say. There was no arguing with her. So I stood with the fridge door open for a few extra seconds, letting the cold air soak in.

"Takes one to know one," teased Grandma as she leaned on the counter. "Shut that fridge, you're letting all the cold out!"

"I'm an angel compared to Lily," I replied sarcastically. As I shut the fridge with a thud and cracked open the soda, just then, my phone buzzed. It was a text from Mom.

"She's almost here!" I yelled in the direction of the hallway.

"Honestly, you couldn't have just walked up there and told them?" Grandma lectured me, turning towards the sink to finish off the last of the dishes.

Moments later both girls came bounding down the stairs, big smiles plastered on their faces as they raced outside to the porch.

After Mom pulled into the driveway I offered to help unload the car, expecting bags of trinkets and gifts piled high from her weekend of shopping. To my dismay there were none, which was odd. All that lay in her trunk was the lonely little suitcase she had taken with her. As I stared at her, puzzled, I realized her gaze held no joy. Instead she looked at me, and it was as if she was staring through me. The sweat on her forehead glossed her pale skin, and the bags under her eyes told me her weekend away had likely been sleepless.

"Hey, how was the trip?" I asked as she got out of the car.

"Oh, you know, the usual. Up all night drinking, talking...typical stuff," she said with a nervous laugh. I watched her struggle up the driveway toward the house, wobbling, almost unable to find her footing. She looked over her shoulder and smiled at me, but I heard her teeth grinding. Unease crept over me, and I knew something was wrong.

"You okay, Mom?" I asked, concern creeped into my voice.

"Yeah, sweetie, I'm okay. Just a headache," she said.

"Can Maya and I go over to Cassie's? Grandma said I had to wait for you to get home," Lily asked, anxiously awaiting approval.

"Go ahead. Have fun."

As Lily and Maya skipped down the block I grabbed Mom's suitcase and followed behind her, leaving it in the foyer along with her shoes and coat. I watched as she flopped down on Dad's oversized recliner, and immediately put her feet up. Her blanched skin looked almost translucent under the harsh, overhead light.

"Mom, maybe you should take a nap. You look wiped out," I said.

She looked at me, her eyes wide and bloodshot. "You're right Nate, I'm exhausted. I just need to lie down. Order pizzas for dinner, okay? Take some cash from my purse to pay the delivery driver." She got up from the chair with a groan. "Maybe after dinner we can have a chat, just me and you. I feel like we never talk anymore."

"Sure Mom," I said. I quickly got my phone out, ordering two pepperoni pizzas with the app before going back to the living room to play some Fortnite. Thirty minutes later the doorbell rang with our dinner, and I put the two boxes in the kitchen. I filled up a plate with steamy slices and retreated back to the living room, excited to devour the food. Not long after Mom walked into the living room to say goodbye to Grandma.

"I feel a lot better," she said. Her eyes were no longer bloodshot, and her skin was now a healthier shade of pink.

"You look a lot better. There is pizza on the kitchen counter."

"Where's your grandmother?" she asked

"In the guest room packing."

She walked toward the front door, fiddling with it before returning and flashing me an odd smile. "You stay right here, Nate. We'll have that chat I promised, but first I need to speak with your grandmother." She proceeded down the hall, her gait a bit more steady than earlier.

"Whatever," I muttered to myself as I heard her open and close the door to Grandma's room.

For a few minutes I forgot they were in there until an unearthly shriek erupted down the hallway. In a panic I rushed to the room, flinging open the door so quickly I stumbled, almost falling over in the process. I watched in horror as Mom pinned Grandma down on the bed, her legs straddling either side of her mother's chest. Mom was trying to grab Grandma's hand, but the older woman was struggling.

That's when I noticed mom was holding something. No, not holding something, more like something was coming out of her hands. I could see them from where I stood, and it was disgusting. They were small, grey worms, and dozens of them were poking their heads out through the palms of her hands.

"Mom," I yelled and rushed towards her ready to tackle her off of Grandma when her gaze locked with mine, stopping me in my tracks. Her eyes were bloodshot, her lips pulled back forming a devilish smile. This was no longer my mother; something else was in control.

"Run!" Grandma shouted from the bed.

I sprinted down the hallway, my footsteps slapping against the hardwood floor. I heard a crash, and when I looked back, the thing in control of my Mom was coming after me.

I ran to the front door and grabbed the handle, trying to force it open, but the door was jammed. I tugged on the handle, pulling it with all the strength I had, but it was useless.

The back door, I remembered and I rushed into the kitchen, but Mom was already there. She was standing in front of the only exit from the house, and I realized that she had planned this.

In desperation I grabbed a knife from the butcher block, waving it maniacally towards her, but she just smiled.

"Get back!" I yelled, holding up the blade to show her I was serious.

"Karen, let the boy go," I heard Grandma plead behind me. It felt like an eternity, but it had only been a minute since I had rushed into the room and my whole world had turned upside down.

"Mom, please, I know you are in there. Wake up. You don't want to do this!" I begged. In response her smile grew wider, and she stepped towards me with her worm-riddled, outstretched hand.

I dropped the knife and grabbed a kitchen chair, hoping to use it to keep her away from me like I had seen a lion tamer do at a circus once. Grandma and I slowly backed towards the living room. My hope that we could get enough distance and smash through a window to get out before she charged again.

I saw Grandma try the doorknob like I had, and she shook her head. Without warning, the door exploded inwards, and the impact threw her to the floor. Her head hitting the hard tile with a loud *crack*. The warm, September air flooded in as I stared at the silhouette of a woman standing before me, gun in hand. I watched in horror as she raised her weapon and aimed it at my mother behind me.

"You can't stop all of us, the ship is built. We're finally getting off this..." Her last words were cut off by the silent bullet that tore through her chest. Her body dropped to the floor beside me with a thud, her warm blood spilling around her as it stained my socks crimson.

"Mom!" I screamed, as I dropped to the floor, discarding the chair as I made my way to her body. "What the Hell are you doing?"

The woman turned towards my Grandma, and without pause shot her in the head.

"Please don't hurt me, I'm just trying to help my mom," I pleaded as I watched in horror as a torrent of beige worms began to spill out of the bullet holes on her chest crawling towards me. Their hard, meal-worm like shelled bodies were coated in her blood.

The woman approached me, her eyes taking in the room. She bent down, careful to avoid the approaching worms.

"Is there anyone else home? Your dad, any siblings?" she asked, her voice trying to be comforting.

"No, my sisters have been away all afternoon and Dad died last year. It's just us," I cried, tears finally escaping my eyes as I lay beside the corpse of the only parent I had left.

"Good," she said, and she turned the gun towards me.

NEILA

It was just another day at the office, and I glared balefully at the tally-filled scoreboard hanging in the cubicle next to mine. Jerry, my least favorite coworker, liked to rub it in everyone's face that he was the best alien hunter in the office, and the scoreboard was his version of proof. I had nearly beat his score last year, but he killed six more aliens than me and won a $10,000 bonus for it. I was going to win this year, and nothing was going to get in my way.

Plus we'd be in the desert, where it'd be easier to kill aliens. Most hated heat, and would only be there if they had to, but it could give us an advantage to beat them. One thing I've learned is that aliens, whether they're Greys or another species, always want something from Earth that we just can't give.

Usually it's a new home or extensive resources, which doesn't sound too bad if they weren't trying to be the dominant species, but sometimes it's a globe full of slaves. My coworkers and I make sure they never attain their goal, and over the decades this line of work has cost more than a few of us our lives.

My latest mission, which was dealing with all of this 'Storm Area 51' bullshit that social media keeps spreading like herpes, has taken longer to prep for than any of us expected. I had been chosen to drive to Nevada and stop any alien I could along the way, so my day just kept getting better and better. It was worth all of the extensive prep work though, because once my files were updated I would get to travel.

I loved being in a different state every time I got an assignment, and driving while listening to horror stories on YouTube was one of my favorite pastimes. I finally finished my data entry, and I was alarmed to find that our research analysts had discovered that the Facebook event was gaining more and more traction as the scheduled day approached. The singular thing that had us all concerned was that, even if only a fifth of the people on Facebook who confirmed that they were going actually showed up, there would still be nearly five-hundred thousand people to deal with.

I would have bet my grandpa's farm that there

would be aliens there, and I was excited to wipe some of the bastards out.

I finally left the office, and I headed out to the car so that I could get to the hotel that had been booked for me. While I loved traveling in general the biggest perk for this trip was my vehicle. The just-released, extremely pricey car came equipped with the latest tech for tracking alien sightings, and with the recent upgrade from my boss Sam the range now covered whichever tri-state area I was in at the time. As soon as I started the car I received notice that a woman had just left Niagara Falls with clear worm marks, and she was headed toward the Baltimore area.

If I left first thing tomorrow my estimate arrival into Baltimore would be in the early evening, which would work well. I loved having my own network of informants who kept me updated on alien sightings, and after having made sure I had at least two of them in each state I knew I could beat Jerry. My little Birdies worked around the clock using software to scan for alien-related Google searches, police reports and visual confirmations of aliens or alien-related markings, and they were also good for hacking into personal information when I needed it. They had discovered that the woman at Niagara had worm-holes in her palms, and I had to remember to send my Birdies a box of cookies when I got back to the office.

After reaching my hotel, and dealing with a very grumpy check-in girl, I threw my stuff on my floor and got my gun ready. By that point my car GPS was loaded with information about the woman, including her address, and I had some general information on her family. Some of her kids were too young to be host bodies, but her eldest child was on the age cusp enough to be an issue.

I quickly made a call, the number used so frequently that I had it memorized. "Leigh-Anne? Hey, it's Neila. I've got a Code 5 at 182 Avendale Row right outside of Baltimore. Five total, but a few are really young, so they probably aren't alien meat-suits. I'm thinking two or three. Yeah, my E.T.A. is around 5 p.m. tomorrow. Be ready on standby."

My office had cleanup crews scattered throughout the country for fast reactions, and it was standard protocol to inform them before a hunt. Without them we would have a lot more bodies to have to make up cover stories for. The next morning I grabbed an untoasted Pop-Tart for the road, then I was headed for the Baltimore outskirts in my wannabe Batmobile. Hours later I found myself at a cute, blue little suburban house a mile outside of the city. I turned off my car, leaving it unlocked in the event that I needed a quick retreat, and made sure that my gun was ready. I had attached the silencer to it before leaving the hotel, and I was prepared in case the infested was on the premises.

All getting into the house took was a single, well-trained kick. It was easy, actually. Shooting the mom was easy. Shooting Granny, who I had accidentally knocked down when I busted through the door, was easy. Shooting the kid? That was damned hard.

"You can't stop all of us. The ship is built, and we're finally getting off this..."

The mother had tried to distract me, to goad me into making a mistake, but I wasn't playing their little games. The most fascinating part of my job is watching the aliens leave the host bodies. Small worms began to spill out of the palms of the mom's hands, and then they began crawling towards me. Their hard, shelled bodies were coated in her blood, and it would have made a typical civilian sick. I was so used to using my boots as weapons that I actually had specialized, reinforced heels that had retractable spikes just for moments like this.

Killing aliens is easy, but talking with the host bodies I have to eliminate can be a bit rough. There've been times, like with the kid lying before me, when I don't want to do this. I was done letting these fucking aliens hurt people. As I stared at the bodies, and the blood sprays speckling the walls, I got mad. I shouldn't have had to kill a kid today, and those bastards would pay for this once I got more of them in sight.

I realized that my phone wasn't in my purse, so I went to my car to retrieve it. Once outside I checked to see if anyone seemed to have heard the commotion, like a nosy neighbour or a police car on patrol, but there were no people on the little cul-du-sac. When I had my phone I headed back inside, my myself comfy on the blood-spattered couch and called Leigh-Anne.

"Hey, me again. Send the crew in, and bring chemicals. Yeah, I think two of the three. Not sure about the boy, but may as well to be safe. Also scan for any potential cameras that might have caught me, or any noise. Thanks."

After clicking my phone shut I waited patiently for a few minutes, and then the mom began to twitch. Her body heaved a few times, like a cat with a hairball, and then I could see it. The worm, the big boss one that had been piloting her, had opened a new hole in her hand, and its slimy ass was wiggling free. I slowly stood, giving it just enough time to plunk to the floor, and then I smashed its face in with the business end of my six-inch stilettos. The crew arrived before I could see the other worms emerge, and I found it fascinating that the bodies sometimes hosted more than a single generation of the little bastards.

Leigh-Anne's crew was as silent as they were effective, and once the biomatter-eating chemicals had been applied to everything there was no trace of blood, bodies, or worms. I didn't envy anyone who had to risk touching the chemicals, and I could only imagine the mishaps that occurred during the testing phase. I thanked them when they finished, and without so much as a glance back I began driving to Nevada. As I passed the van they had come in I nearly chuckled: this group of Leigh-Anne's was undercover as 'Worms Be Gone Pest Control'.

How original.

I gave my boss a call, informing a pleased Sam of another successful hunt, and then activated my scanner. I was running ahead of schedule, and had plenty of time to stop if any more of these bastards were sighted near me. Plus it gave me time to listen to the latest horror story uploads from Swamp Dweller and Darkness Prevails, which would at least make me a little happy after such a shitty day.

ELAIN

I was jostled awoke hours later, headlights streaked past the darkness beyond the window. Shit! The camper was no longer parked; we were on the road, and moving quickly. Had someone stolen the camper? How long had I slept? I could hear hushed voices from the front over the sounds of the highway, but couldn't make them out.

A piercing screech broke through their mumbled words, and I recognized that sound as the walkie-talkies we had gotten the boys for Christmas last year.

The walkie-talkies were handheld, two-way radios with a pretty significant range. I remembered how they had eagerly ripped the packaging open, and immediately ran to test them. Adrienne had dashed downstairs to the basement to see if they would work underground, while Thomas went running to the creek about a half-mile away. The gift was a success, and by the end of the night they were getting full signal from nearly a mile away.

"Can you hear me? Over." The heavy static voice coming through the walkie talkie sounded like my brother William.

"We can read you loud and clear. Over," my mother answered. A wave of relief washed over me as I realized I hadn't inadvertently been kidnapped by a car thief, just taken for a joyride by my unobservant parents. They apparently hadn't realized I was in the back. I prepared to yell out a greeting when what William said next instantly silenced me.

"Did you have any issues at the Sarnia border crossing?"

Border crossing... Sarnia? What the Hell? Are we in the States?!

"No. We went into lane six like you told us, and the patrol officer waved us through just like expected. Over.".

"Excellent. Over."

"Anyone heard from Elain yet? Over." I heard

Ashley's voice screech over the speaker. She must have been with them in the other car. What the fuck was going on?

"Not yet. We left Thomas and Adrien to take Greg to the beach for processing. They will find her, and make their way to Area 51 and meet us there. Over."

Oh my god, Trevor!

I couldn't contain my gasp as the situation came crashing down on me. I didn't know what was going on, and I didn't know what they meant by processing, or why we were suddenly going to Area 51; none of this was making any sense. All I knew was I needed to get out of there now. I needed to get to Trevor.

"Shit, she's in here," my Dad said. I was thrown against the side of the camper as he quickly swerved over to the side of the highway, my head smashing into the corner of the bathroom door. Pain seared through my head. I put my hand up to my forehead, and it was wet. Shit, was that blood? Was I bleeding?

The curtains were yanked open, my parents' forms looming over me. They moved towards me, and I shuffled backwards until I could go no further, hitting the side of the small bed.

"Mom, what's going on?" I began, but they ignored me.

"Hold her down," Mom yelled, her voice deranged. Before I had time to process what was happening, Dad leapt at me, his eyes mad and wild. I had never seen him like that before. I had no time to react.

Mom jumped on me next, her arms stretched out towards me. She had red pinprick marks on the palm of her hands, just like Pierce had, except hers were growing larger. I watched as they changed, dilating and opening into dozens of holes. Small beige worms with large heads and small pinchers began inching their way out. She grabbed my hand, placed her festering palm on mine, and I felt them seeking me. The worms were burrowing into my hand! Each was a quick pin prick, and then nothing but numbness, and within seconds my entire palm was numb to the onslaught.

I kicked and screamed, trying to wrestle myself away, but it was no use. Darkness crept around the corner of my eyes and my body, which had been full of adrenaline moments ago, was now exhausted. My eyes began to close, and the world around me slowly started to fade away.

"There, all done. She will wake up feeling like a new person in the morning." Their manic laughter, unfamiliar and terrifying, was the last thing I heard before the darkness consumed me.

PART 3

SEPTEMBER 17, 2019

K *A-THUD!* "Gahh! Fuck!" I hissed to myself. My sciatica sent a bolt of lightning down my right leg as the bus skipped over a pothole. I don't know if I was more frustrated by the pain, or by the fact that I didn't anticipate the same damn pothole this bus has been hitting every day for the past fourteen years.

Whoa. Has it really been fourteen years?

I looked down at the badge hanging around my neck: "Biological Optimization Technician. United States Air Force." I used to be so proud of this badge. I shifted my focus to the clear, plastic badge-holder it was neatly slipped into. It wasn't clear anymore, and was turning yellow with age. I glanced around the bus at a few of my co-workers' badge-holders, which were all crystal clear.

Have I really been here that long, or do I just need a new badge holder?

We rounded the last corner of our journey, which meant we only had a few minutes left. Although I couldn't see the road, or the surrounding mountainscape beyond the blacked out windows of the bus, I knew we were almost to Area 51. Well, technically we had already driven through Area 51. The bus was taking us to Site S-4, the secret facility within the Area 51 gates. It's so secret that they decided to carve the entire thing, airplane hangars and all, out of the side of a mountain so it couldn't be spied on from space. The non-disclosure agreement I signed years ago still scared me enough never to mention where I worked or what I did to anyone, not even my wife. She left me because of it.

Believe it or not, the U.S. Government's public stance on the facility itself is actually true. Its primary function is to serve as an advanced, military aircraft testing facility, but anyone who's ever been cursed enough to hop on that S-4 bound, darkened bus knew that there was so much more inside. Site S-4 was where the U.S. Government conducted the study of extraterrestrial technology and lifeforms, mainly on live subjects. That's right, S-4 is where they keep the aliens.

As a Molecular Biologist and a top scientist at S-4, and I was assigned to study and understand the physical relationship between the extraterrestrial lifeforms we refer to as the "Taus", and the human race. Let's just say our relationship is...complicated.

It all started with the infamous crash in Roswell, New Mexico in 1947. I don't think anyone actually believes the whole "crashed weather balloon" schtick the government peddles. It was indeed an extraterrestrial craft that crashed, and there were indeed three "Grey Aliens" inside. Only, the Greys were already dead -- long dead -- and crawling around the outside of the ship were hundreds of small, beige-colored, worm-like creatures who were very much alive.

These little worms, the Taus (we deduced their origin to be from the Tau Ceti system, although they never confirmed it), had invaded the bodies of the Greys and controlled their higher brain functions. They had borrowed deep inside their central nervous systems and used nerve endings as information pathways. The host bodies were reduced to housing units for the Taus, a husk used to perform physical tasks requiring strength, explore space, and communicate with other species in a more granular form. And among the wreckage were the bodies of the humans whom happened upon the crash before the Government clean up crew arrived. Unconscious and infested with Taus, just like the Greys.

The Taus are truly fascinating creatures. They're all about two inches in length and no more than a half-inch in total circumference. They have no distinctive physical features besides a semi-hard shell, small sharp pinchers and only a few crude internal organs. Their bodies are sensitive to heat and can't sustain life above 104° F. From a biological standpoint they're so simple that a grad student could dissect one and tell you exactly what's inside, but in their physical simplicity lies their infinite complexity. Like most things during my time at Area 51, this was initially shown to me rather than told.

Like most things during my time at Area 51, this was initially shown to me rather than told. During one of my first days on the job fourteen years ago, my boss, whom I only ever saw once a week and was known only to me as "Director Magruder", walked me past our lab to a series of holding cells. Inside one of the cells, wearing nothing but a hospital gown, was a middle-aged man kneeling on the ground facing the back corner. Magruder explained to me that this man's name was Carl, and that he was quite special. He rapped on the glass wall of the cell and Carl instinctively shot up and faced us. I remember this day as if it was yesterday......

"Good morning, Carl. I'd like you to meet someone," said Magruder.

The man inside the glass cell named Carl had a quizzical look on his face as he slowly paced towards the glass. He didn't stop until his ruddy, snot-ridden nose was about a centimeter away from the glass. His eyes were on me, but he wasn't looking at me. He was looking through me.

"Hello Magruder. Who is guest you've brought to visit me." Carl said with a sneer.

Unable to respond introducing myself, due to the sheer creepiness of the environment I found myself in, I waited for Magruder to break the silence.

"Carl, this is Gerald. He's here to help you. He's here to learn about you and help make your time with us here on Earth as tolerable as possible." Magruder turned to me. "Gerald, this is Carl; however he is also one of The Taus" I turned confused eyes towards Magruder, not understanding what he was implying. "The body of the man you see before you once had the legal name of Carl Gehringer. But this body is no longer Carl Gehringer's, it's now occupied by a Taus.

The Taus acts as a parasite inside that man's central nervous system, controlling his every movement, every word, and every breath. It's in there, along with a hundred of its little friends."

I looked back at Magruder with an expression that silently screamed, You're fucking kidding me. The man in the cell, Carl, kept blankly staring through me.

Magruder continued, "The Taus have been on this planet, and subsequently at this facility, for the past 58 years. We've learned a considerable amount of information about them in that time, but there's still so much we don't understand." As he walked towards the glass, Carl ignored him, continuing to stare through me. "We still don't understand how a creature as small as a common mealworm has the ability to enter the body of a host, invade its central nervous system, and single-handedly take it over."

He didn't stop walking until his nose was about a centimeter from his side of the glass wall. Carl and Magruder were standing face to face, less than two inches apart, but it felt like there were miles between them. "But we have at least cultivated a... humane way to study them."

Magruder would go on to explain that only a handful of original Taus from the 1947 crash were left, and this particular Tau inside of Carl's body was their leader. They had a social hierarchy that we didn't understand, but we did know this Tau had uncanny abilities to retain host body memories and was somewhere in the neighborhood of 250 years old. As I would discover, Magruder's "humane" way of studying Taus was by forcibly terminating the human host body so the Tau could jump to another. The name Carl had stuck with the Area 51 team, and hence it stuck with this particular Tau, even through it occupied a dozen or so hosts while in captivity.

For fourteen years, I would lie in bed awake at night and think about how this tiny, alien creature had taken this man Carl Gehringer's life, his body and his name.

Whenever I asked Carl how the Taus were able to take over bodies he would always reply with some variation of "your language doesn't have sufficient enough words for it". So, instead of describing it, I just forced him to do it over and over and over again. I observed that the way Taus entered and exited human bodies was through the palms, feet, and armpits. They had the ability to burrow through the pores of human sweat glands, forcibly navigate their way to the central nervous system, and then latch onto the brain stem between the pons and the medulla. Their tiny bodies would send electrical signals to the human brain that would mimic motor functions almost perfectly, and they could even access the host's short-term memory. From a sheer scientific perspective the manifestation of this process was beyond a molecular biologist's wildest dreams, and from a moral perspective it was sadistic torture for the hosts.

Long before I got to Area 51 my superiors had established a practice of acquiring various *live* human host bodies, solely for the purpose of understanding the Taus' takeover process. One day, about a year into my time here, Magruder told me that we would be conducting a "transition" on Carl. The two of us, along with three men in military uniforms, went to Carl's holding cell, drugged him, put him in a wheelchair, and wheeled him into an operating room. Already in the operating room were three surgeons wearing lab coats, masks, and latex gloves. They placed Carl face-down on an operating table, then they made a small incision in the back of his neck. Using a suction device, which looked almost like a turkey baster, they were able to pull the tiny Tau out of the host body and deposit it into a glass beaker. Carl's worm-like body writhed frantically within the beaker, splattering blood and viscera all over the glass. Meanwhile the surgeons lifted up a sheet that was draped over an adjacent operating table, which revealed the face-down body of a scraggly-haired woman with sun-cracked skin. They made a small incision in the back of her neck, sucked Carl back into the same device and shoved him into the central nervous system of the new host. The woman was unconscious, and after a few hours Carl, through the host body, came to and started speaking to us as if nothing had ever happened.

For the next fourteen years (*Jesus. It really HAD been fourteen years...*), I had somehow been able to look past all of this. I stared through all of the heinous experimentation, and all of the utter Hell this job had unleashed on my emotional health and my personal life. Everything was in service to a greater cause, to the advancement of science. As a coping mechanism to rationalize the carnage which was being left in my wake I had to constantly remind myself that I was on the cutting edge of scientific discovery. I told myself it was for the best when my wife left me, and that it wasn't realistic to expect anyone to be married to a man who had sold his soul the way I did. I had, over the years, built up emotional walls against the thousands of logical and moral mortars being hurled at me from all angles.

Until today. The day they asked me to go too far. The walls I had worked so hard to construct for so long came crashing down the instant I looked into her eyes.

Waiting for me in the lab was Director Magruder, his hands resting on the shoulders of a little girl. She couldn't have been more than seven years old. She had shoulder-length brown hair, and was wearing dirty overalls and sneakers that used to be white. Huge, brown eyes stared helplessly up at me, and she was too scared to cry. I don't know what my face looked like, but I can't imagine it had been masking my emotions. I knew exactly what Director Magruder was going to say before he said it.

"Gerald, meet the new Carl."

My pulse quickened, and my heart started pounding out of my chest.

"As you know, Tau B-293 expired this morning, after its reassignment along with its host. So our good friend Carl is the last one. Our last opportunity to understand."

Magruder tightened his grip on the girl's shoulders. I could see the whites of his knuckles as his bony fingers clung to her.

"And it's not every day we arrive at this... incredible opportunity. An opportunity to observe a Tau in this... younger, more fresh environment."

Magruder swung his head down to face the girl's left ear, his voice practically a hiss.

"I want to move fast, Gerald. We have one Tau left. The time for questions is over. I want answers. The bosses want answers. You can make it work. Right Gerald?"

I didn't make a sound. Magruder snaked his head back up, looking at me with all the zeal of a cult leader who had already passed out the Kool-Aid. "Gerald, this is a new frontier!"

I felt my sciatica flare, which typically only happens when my body gets jostled, but the realization of what I was about to do physically struck me. I opened my mouth to speak, but all that came out was a breathy croak. The last, tiny spark of my soul was being sucked out. Over the last fourteen years my soul, little by little, had withered. Surely, after this, there would be nothing left.

ELAIN

9:12 A.M.

I t was morning. Or maybe afternoon, I couldn't really tell. Light streamed through the small window above me, and the camper was eerily silent and still so we must have parked somewhere.

I bit my lip, trying to suppress a groan as I struggled to get up, my head pounding from where I had hit the wall last night.

My hands felt like they were on fire. I looked down, and I noticed that the palms of my hands were swollen. They were covered in what looked like large, festering bumps, almost like blisters that had burst. I examined my hands, poking into the sores. Memories from the night before came flooding back. My parents screaming and holding me down, worms wriggling out of their hands, and them pushing the creatures onto me. It wasn't a dream, it had been real.

I ran to the bathroom, dry heaving bile into the small toilet. The palms of my hands began to burn, and soon I could feel the worms began to drip out of the gaping wounds. Their lifeless husks were unmoving as they hit the bathroom floor with wet thuds.

What the fuck!

I wanted to scream and cry, curl up into a little ball and sleep this nightmare away, but I couldn't. These things had been inside of me and for whatever reason, be it the remaining radiation of the medication that I was on, my body had killed them before they could take over. I almost laughed as I watched the last of them fall out of my bloodied hand. I crushed one under my foot, watching with satisfaction as its small body burst open like a pomegranate seed. In a rage I began stomping on them, grinding into the vinyl flooring until they were nothing but a wet paste.

What the fuck are these things? A parasite that infects people, causing violent tendencies? I had seen Pierce the other night, and now my parents. Whatever was going on they were no longer safe to be around, and I wasn't going to stick around and see if they were feeling any better this morning. I needed to get out of there.

My hands were still sore, but it looked like there weren't any more worms spilling out of the wounds. I quickly washed my hands, wrapping them in a washcloth I found under the small cupboard, and quietly made my way out of the bathroom.

Moving towards the door I peered out of the window, and the coast was clear. I couldn't see anyone, and it looked like we had parked the camper behind a row of older buildings. I quickly jumped out, quietly shut the door, and ran towards a small alleyway. I figured I was headed towards the main road, but just as I took a step I saw William and my parents round the corner. I ducked behind a garbage bin, pulling old, greasy cardboard boxes over me in the hope that they would hide me well enough.

"When are we all meeting at the gate?" My mother asked. Her soft voice made me want to crawl out from underneath the cardboard and run into her arms, but that wasn't my mother. Not anymore.

"The event on Facebook says to meet on September 20th, so that's in three days," William said.

"Do we know how many of us will be there yet?" Dad asked, his voice getting louder as they drew closer.

"We haven't gotten a final count, but the event posted on the facebook shows hundreds of thousands of humans are planning to attend. Some are even bringing camera crews and broadcasting the whole thing," William said. They were right in front of me now. I could see him carrying a tray of coffee and a brown paper bag. *What the hell is going on, were they out getting breakfast like it's just a normal Tuesday?*

"I still can't believe that worked, by the way. Thank goodness for technological hysteria. After years of trying to get into Area 51 ourselves, we may have finally found a way into the facility. Get the humans to break through the gates for us!" my mother crowed.

"I don't know. This government doesn't normally let people get away with this kind of force," I could hear my dad warn, his tone familiar.

"They aren't going to shoot at thousands of their own. Once the gates are open, we should be able to follow the mob in and get our family out," William insisted.

"You never know. Do you know how long they've

kept this secret?" I could hear Dad say, their voices now much harder to hear.

"Do we even have a choice anymore? This is our last chance to get them before we leave. What do they call him again?" I could hear William ask.

I strained to hear the answer, but it was to no avail. They were out of earshot, and there was no way of getting closer without giving away my location. Bits and pieces from the conversation last night and what I was able to overhear now finally started making sense. This wasn't a parasite. As absurd as it was, this was a fucking *alien* invasion. They were using us as hosts, crawling into our bodies and taking over. Becoming us. I had to tell someone.

From the slit in the cardboard I could see them open the front door of the camper and step inside. This was my chance. I stood up, letting the cardboard fall off of me, and ran out of the alley. A shout echoed behind me as I rounded the corner, but I didn't stop.

I found the small police station a few blocks away, across from the impressive city hall that towered over the small shops and apartment buildings in the area.

I entered the cool building and looked around, trying to figure out where I should go, when I saw a small woman in the far corner stand up from behind a massive desk and wave me over. I quickly walked towards her, my breath slowly becoming normal. I watched her run to a small office behind her desk, and a moment later she emerged with a young-looking police woman that took one look at me before nodding towards the receptionist.

"Excuse me," I began, but was cut off.

"Just sit right in here miss, we'll take your statement in this area." She spoke softly. Her name tag read Officer Hudson. "It's a private room, and we'll have someone with you in a moment."

A glance at a passing window beside me confirmed my suspicions. The mirrored surface reflected a woman who looked like she had walked in off the streets after an attack. Dried blood streaked down from my forehead, seeping into my clothing. The shoulder of my tank top had been torn sometime during the scuffle, and it exposed the white, lace bra underneath.

The small room held just a small, round table and two chairs. I was ushered towards the far chair and told to sit and wait, but sitting was impossible. Adrenaline from the run here, as well as from the previous night's terror, flooded my body. The nervous energy had me pacing the small room, madly counting my steps while I waited for the officer to arrive.

Three hundred and twenty six steps later a pudgy officer opened the door. He was holding a large writing pad and pen, and his tie was stained and crooked. He eyed me warily before taking a seat at the chair closest to the door, and he motioned for me to sit.

"What's your name, please," he began. His tone was already annoyed and rushed, as if I was an inconvenience to his day.

"My name is Elain Roberts," I said, my brain still scattered. I sat quickly, trying to calm my shaking hands in front of me.

"Who did this to you?" he said, his eyes never leaving the blank page.

"What? No, that's not what I'm here about. They have my son," I began, my words coming out choppy and confused.

He looked up at that, his mud-brown eyes searching my face. "Who has your son?"

"They do, my husband. But he isn't my husband anymore." I was starting to panic. "No, this is coming out wrong."

"Ma'am, are you saying your husband attacked

you and took your son?" he asked, looking slightly more interested.

"No, no. I was attacked last night by my parents. But they aren't my parents anymore. Look, these are wounds caused by some sort of worm they tried to infect me with..." I ripped the towels from my hands, trying to show him the redness still scaring my palms, but he rolled his eyes.

"Worms, great. We have another one!" he shouted over his shoulder towards the closed door.

"No, you don't understand," my voice was now raised, and fear began to take over. "They drove me over the border last night, and then they attacked me. I only woke up this morning and realized I was in the States."

"Ma'am, are you saying you entered the country illegally?" His voice was grim.

"That isn't what this is about. They have my son!"

"Where's your passport?"

"You aren't listening, and why aren't you writing any of this down? I was attacked last night, in my parents' camper. I overheard them say that they were going to take my son to a town called Rachel, you need to..."

"Look, Elain Roberts, that's your name right?

Elain?" he said, cutting me off. He looked angry now, no longer indifferent.

"Yes, that's my name."

"Elain, I need you to stay right here."

"But..." I stood up as I watched him move towards the door, his hand already turning the handle.

"Sit down, and stay put," he said.

"Can you at least put out an Amber Alert, or let the authorities in Rachel know to look for him? I have photos on my phone. I can give you a photo," I grabbed my phone from my pocket, trying to open the screen, but my thumbprint was wet with sweat.

"Elain, sit down. You just admitted you crossed the border and are in the country illegally. Your son is the least of your concerns, now sit. Stay," he demanded, like I was a dog who needed to be put in her place.

He walked through the door, closing it loudly. I could hear his heavy footprints make their way down the hall. I jumped and tested the handle, and it wasn't locked. I counted to 10, held my breath, and ran through the door, making it out of the police station before anyone took notice.

Thankfully I still had my cell phone and my wallet with me. I might not have had any American cash, but at least I had credit cards and an Uber app. I was going to follow my son, but first I needed to rent myself a vehicle. If the police weren't going to help me, I was going to find Trevor myself, and figure out what the hell was happening to my family.

I could feel the blazing sun beat down on me, like the eternal fires of Hell. My pale arms were burning under the assault of the desert sun.

We were in the middle of fucking nowhere; the only thing around was sand, sand and- oh, more god damn sand. The gates, as they were so-called, were very underwhelming if you took out the military presence. They were located at the end of a long road, miles away from the Extraterrestrial highway and the little town of Rachel, Nevada. A high chain-link fence carved a line into the desert as far as your eyes could see. The "gates" themselves were a simple black and white arm, one you would see in a parking garage that needed someone to press a button to lift up, with a guard station attached. So the place was basically a fancy garage. What lay beyond the gates was Area 51. Miles away, too far to be seen, was what we were there for. We just needed to walk through and see it.

They had warned me the climate change from Alaska to Nevada would put me through the wringer, and as much as I had prepared myself mentally there was no getting around how goddam fucking hot it was. The heat literally radiated from the desert sand beneath our feet, making it feel like we were in a brick oven. By noon I had completely soaked through my sports bra and my "the truth is HERE" t-shirt that Craig had made for the group.

Thank goodness it was black, or else the sweat rings would have been even more embarrassing than wearing the giant safari hat that Pat had made me bring. I had no intention of using it, and I hated how its wide brim extended past my shoulders, with a small netting held up by strings that acted like a sail when the wind was right. Even so, after only twenty minutes in the desert sun I had relented against my fashion sense and chosen the more practical route: keep as much sun off of me, and look like an idiot doing it.

"Hey Carrie, how's it going?" I saw Craig emerge

from the large crowd gathered to the west of the Gate.

I met Craig, along with his sister Heather and the rest of our online community, last night when I rolled into town. There was Tom and Nick, who came from California with their large class A motorhome. It had all the comforts of city living on wheels, including a huge air conditioner that kept the camper so cold it felt like you were walking into a meat locker. Most of the crew, when not handing out flyers or talking with the unbelievers, were holed up in there staying cool.

By the time I had arrived the group had already set up camp about a mile from the gate itself. I smiled as I drove through the mass of tents already set up, and saw a "the truth is HERE" sign at the edge of camp, showing me the way home. There were twelve trailers in total so far, but I expected many more would arrive shortly. We had all parked around a large meeting space in the center that had been left open, and there were picnic tables with umbrellas and a large fire pit. It made the makeshift trailer park feel cozy and welcoming.

"Oh you know me, just sweating my balls off trying to talk sense into these stupid kids," I said, pointing to the group of barely twenty-year-olds huddled in a circle with hardly any clothes on, passing a joint between them. "Seriously, put on some sunscreen!" I shouted towards them.

One... two ... three ...

Craig chuckled, his wide smile shadowed from the shade of the umbrella he was carrying. He had had a few of them made for the event, each stamped with the same logo as our t-shirts, buttons, and flyers. Sweat was collecting on his upper lip, and I watched as he nervously wiped it away with the back of his gloved hand.

I had thought the gloves were unusual last night. When I was shaking hands with everyone, them with their black gloves and me with my sweaty palms, I just mentally shrugged. When I asked about it they had told me it was for hygienic reasons, and after seeing someone take a piss where they stood by the gates I totally got it. This place was disgusting. I might just ask if they had an extra pair they could give me for the rest of the week. If the government didn't kill us on the way in through the gates I was sure we were all going to die of some awful desert parasite, mainly because no one had washed their hands this entire week.

"Hi Craig, looks like you handed a few out," I

said, noticing his stack was about half the size of mine already.

"Yes I did, had a good talk with a few of the Unbelievers as well. I even had a dozen or so agree to come to our meeting tonight. Talk about the truth, spread the word." His smile grew wider at that, and I couldn't help but smile back. His excitement was infectious, and for good reason.

For months we had been planning this trip. Face-Timing back and forth, discussing our plan of attack. It was simple really, a method used time and time again. Talk to people, face to face. We would spread out each day with our informational flyers and smiles and educate those that gathered at the gates about the realities the government has been hiding from them for years. We would tell them about the conspiracy the government has been keeping from its own citizens for years, and some of them would embrace the truth.

Tonight was going to be our first big meeting, with some outsiders joining, and I know everyone was excited. We could only hope that, by inviting these groups in and sharing about our own painful experiences, they would band with us and demand entrance into the facility.

Our goal was to have enough citizens backing us

that the government wouldn't be able to stop us once we were through the gates. They would have no choice but to let us through, or risk killing every one of us.

I looked around the gate, amazed at the crowd that had amassed overnight. Even in the heat of the day throngs of people were walking around, hiding under small shade tents or just laying out suntanning.

Already I could see three groups forming.

The Truth Seekers, like myself, who were there to protest at the gate and spread the truth about government conspiracy.

The Unbelievers, as we liked to call them, who came to the gate expecting a party. They had been slowly trickling in a few dozen at a time over the last hour or so, backpacks at the ready and one lone water bottle in hand. Some had been smart enough to bring some shade tents to hide under during the day, but most were completely unprepared for the desert conditions. The lack of sanitary bathrooms and fresh water bordered on dangerous already, and I could only imagine how bad it was going to get in the next few days. Luckily, for those that wanted to join our camp, we had set up a water station for anyone needing to refill their bottles and plenty of shade in our meeting space.

The last group was the Government Drones. They had stationed themselves as close to the gates as the military would allow, and they were taking the stand that they were there to protect the government and keep us out. They mainly consisted of retired army and military, but had a fair number of regular citizens mixed in as well set to keep the facility's secrets just that: secret. They were the extreme survivalists, and they patrolled the civilian side of the gate with guns strapped to their backs. They arrived much like ourselves, with trailers and campers equipped with ACs and supplies, ready and willing to stay for as long as it took.

"What's going on over there?" I heard Craig say, and I turned towards his outstretched hand.

A small crowd had gathered in the Drone section, a small figure barely visible in the center of the huddled mass.

"Is that Heather?" I asked, moving towards the group. Their collective voices began to get louder as we approached.

Before I knew it a yelp cut through the air and Heather was on the ground, her flyers tossed into the air and raining down around them.

"Get the fuck out of here, you crazy bitch," I heard a giant of a man yell at Heather, her small frame crouched underneath his overbearing mass.

Shouts of approval came from the crowd around him.

I elbowed my way into the circle and grabbed Heather by her gloved hand, moving her behind me. Her eyes were wet with tears, and they were wide with fright.

"What the fuck is wrong with you?" I yelled at the ringleader, his handlebar mustache and wife beater shirt making me hate him even more. Could he look anymore like a stereotypical asshole?

"We don't want any of you crazy nut-bags anywhere near us!"

"So you decided to attack her?" I moved closer, our bodies almost touching now. I could see the sweat accumulating on his forehead, his face hot with rage.

ONE..TWO..THREE..FOUR..FIVE..SIX..SEVEN

"I didn't touch the fucking bitch. Told her to get her ass out of here but she wouldn't listen. Just kept sticking those goddamn flyers in our faces, wanting to take us back to her trailer and show us something."

Craig stood beside me now, holding Heather protectively while the group of Drones got closer, flocking to protect their leader from a lady in a silly hat. Fuck, they were stupid.

"I don't care what she did, she has every right to be here. It's our right to protest the government and demand answers." I grabbed a handful of flyers on the ground. "Are you afraid of the truth? Are you afraid of little girls and their flyers?"

"Take your slut friend home and get out of here, you crazy bitch!" He screamed at my face. His spittle sprayed me with the force of his words as he jabbed his finger into my chest.

ONETWOTHREFOURFIVESIXSEV-ENEIGHTNINETEN

He touched me first, and they all saw it.

"I am so sick of people calling me CRAZY!" I screamed, cocking my arm back and punching the asshole squarely in the jaw, the force of the punch rattling my arm. He stumbled back, his hand reaching up and rubbing his injured face.

Strong arms caught me around my waist, dragging me away from the gathering crowd. I struggled against the restraint, yelling obscenities as curious observers watched on.

"Relax Carrie, it's me," I immediately stopped fighting, realizing it wasn't one of the Drones touching me, but Craig. He was hurrying us back to our campers.

"You keep that crazy bitch away from us, you hear!" the asshole shouted as we rounded the corner of the trailer.

I refrained from running back and leaping at him again, knowing we were outnumbered and outgunned.

"That group is going to be trouble," Craig said as we made our way back.

"They better just stay out of my way. I didn't come all this way to be pushed around by a group of government Drones. We're getting through that gate, one way or another, and we deserve answers."

"Don't worry Carrie. We'll get through, no matter what," His tone was serious, and I liked that.

"No matter what," I echoed.

We walked back to my camper, the heat and the encounter with the Drones enraging me to the point that I was starting to feel dizzy. I needed to cool down, drink some water, and regroup. I wasn't going to let a group of idiots keep us from exposing the truth. We needed to figure out a new plan, a way through the Drones guarding the gate. And to do that, we would need guns. Lots of them.

All I want is to stop these damned aliens from taking over our planet, but more and more just kept popping up. I had made it as far as Utah before my scanner pinged, and I ended up taking a fun little detour. My tech had picked up a phone call to a therapist, and it was a woman talking about her rich, cheating husband. She had said that he had been acting strange lately, and that he had weird little pinpricks in his hands. She suspected it was some sort of new way to shoot up cocaine, but I knew better. She said that he would be reaching their private airport soon when he returned from a 'business trip', and I knew what I'd be doing.

After a quick hack job by one of my Birdies I had the information I needed, and I easily reached the tiny, private landing strip that the affluent couple owned. I made my usual call to Leigh-Anne, and when his plane arrived I was ready. I had even applied a bit of makeup to look like one of the hookers his email said he was paying for, just so he wouldn't immediately suspect anything. The businessman, and a group of scantily-clad women, came down the boarding steps. The first thing out of his mouth made me want to punch him.

"Hey sexy, I didn't realize I had left one of you behind."

I could practically smell the alcohol from where I stood, but I played coy until I could get close enough to check his palms. I twirled a finger through one of my wavy, auburn locks, a pout gracing my lips.

"I just couldn't wait to see you, so I thought I would meet you here! You didn't have too much fun without me, did you?"

The asshat didn't even question how I knew where to find him.

"Nononooooo baby, there's plenty of fun still left! Right girls!? Let's show her some fun! I needed a chick with some more curves, this bunch is kinda frail for our liking."

He stretched his hands out towards me, like a baby to a bottle, and as he took a few shaky steps forward I could see all that I needed to. The tell-tale, evenly-spaced pinpricks were there, and if that wasn't enough his creepy use of 'our' would have queued me in. Before he could react my fist shot out on instinct, connecting squarely with his jaw and making the satisfying crunch that signaled broken bones.

My gun took care of the rest.

After I shot the businessman, and then his pilot, two of his four exotic companions tried to rush me. I had fought people who were better trained than them though, and they were no match for me. A jab to the stomach here, an elbow to the nose there, and all was well. I was extra careful not to make any skin contact, and my thick, leather duster protected me from some of their blows, so I came out in pretty good shape.

Just like with the boy's family I did my little worm curb-stomp routine, and when I finished I had a nice bit of adrenalin-fueled satisfaction coursing through my veins. As I wiped the extraterrestrial blood off of my boots I realized that, in just two days, I had taken out over half a dozen worms and their hosts, making that close to a hundred worms by my count. This was more than some agents managed in a year, and I wasn't done yet. Thanks to the mother alien I knew that there would be more of them at the Storming event, and I was ready to up my alien body count.

I was stepping over the last dead host, one of the hookers, when her necklace caught my eye. I halted, staring down at the tiny, blue stone surrounded by silver flowers.

It was just like my mother's necklace.

I stared hard at the corpse for a minute, willing myself to look away. I hadn't seen that style of necklace since I had to kill my mom, a little over a decade ago. I was sixteen when she got infected by a Tau, and that was what had kickstarted my career as an alien hunter. I never forgot her manic smile, or they way her eyes were disturbingly bloodshot. Like any infection there was some unpredictability, but I would later learn that those were common symptoms for the first day or two usually.

She had tried to put some of those disgusting, fucking worms inside of me, and in my terror I had bashed her over the head with the urn that held my grandmother's ashes.

When the extraterrestrial cleanup crew came into my house, barely ten minutes after my mother drew her last breath, I was curled on the floor sobbing. They clearly hadn't expected me to be there, which in hindsight wasn't a surprise. I was usually at my grandpa's on weekends, but had come home early because I had gotten food poisoning. That was the day Taylor, Sam's predecessor, had introduced herself to me. I went to live with my grandpa, and a few years later she took me on as a trainee. I worked under her for about three years, until she got killed in action. A group of Greys had caught her alone, and they overwhelmed her with sheer numbers.

I didn't have time for this sentimental shit. I needed to get going, and I had a mission to focus on.

Later that day I finally reached Nevada, and I was in my latest hotel when my tablet, which I had just finished rewiring so it could receive info from the car scanner, pinged. I was feeling pretty exhausted, and I didn't immediately look at the alien-related information that had been added to the internet. I slept for a few hours, finally catching up on the rest that I was sorely lacking, but my dreams were bombarded with red sunsets and living squiggles. Later that night I finally opened the tablet notification, and I was immediately interested. This time it was a police case from the Davenport Jail in Nevada, and it seemed like the war gods were smiling upon me.

An APB for a woman named Elain Roberts had gone out, and it seemed like she had filed a report saying that she had seen worms coming from the palms of her family member's hands. She claimed that they had kidnapped her young son, and were headed to Area 51 for the Storming event. After reading the information I figured that she would be heading to the desert to find her family, and if I trailed her, she would lead me right into another group of aliens. Jerry could kiss my rack and buy me a bourbon, because my score was about to kick his score's ass.

RANDY

8:45 P.M.

hy are rest stop restrooms always so dingy? I shook my hands dry as I pushed the door open, walking out into the growing darkness. *Does no one clean them?* I began thinking about a way to work that onto a shirt. Maybe a bathroom for cars?

I pondered the possibilities. *Something something tailpipe...* As I walked back to the parking lot I slung my backpack over my shoulder. It was one of those cheap canvas things with the fold-over tops, in that ugly camo-green color. It had been literally one of a hundred identical bags on the rack at that large, chain department store. You know the one. I had loaded up some snacks and a change of clothes, along with a few toiletries. I always believe in packing light. It was the desert, so how much could I possibly need?

I began looking for someone who would be able to take me on the next leg of the trip. Due to having to redo some artwork I'd not been able to leave as early as I'd hoped, but I knew I had given myself plenty of time to get there. I figured I should try and get part of the way that night to get a jump on it, so all I needed to find was someone heading up the 14. It was bad luck that the first guy I rode with was heading up to Oregon, but I guess I should have expected a few bumps when I decided to hitch instead of taking the bus. Isn't there some saying about choosy hitchers? Probably something about being horribly murdered...

Suddenly my heart stopped. I couldn't believe my eyes. At the end of the row stood a long-legged brunette, and she had the hottest curves I had ever seen. She was leaning against a shiny, black Sonata. I quickly checked my hair in the nearest rear-view mirror, its sandy blonde highlights still had the "fresh from the beach" look. Perfect. I started forward, standing as tall as my 5'6" would allow. She began climbing into her car as I approached.

I cleared my throat. "Excuse me Miss, are you heading to..."

"Nope." The door slammed shut.

Her loss.

As she drove off I saw movement in the back of one of the nearby cars, and I snickered as I realized what I was seeing. A small woman in a green tank top was straddling the man with her, staring into his eyes. They were doing the Tarzan hand thing, hands held palm-to-palm. Slowly her fingers began to curl in between his, and his eyes closed. When her own eyes began to roll back into her head I knew that I had seen more than enough. I thought about rapping on the window and telling them to get a room, but decided to just keep looking.

Unfortunately the elderly couple in the handicapped spot were also going north on the 5. The bearded guy in the Buick looked like a real possibility, until I saw the little girl in his backseat. A chill ran up my spine as hours of Frozen sing-alongs flashed before my eyes.

That just left the battered pick-up in the back corner of the lot. As I approached I saw through the open window that the driver, a small man with a baseball cap pulled down over his face, was slumped back in his seat. I sighed inwardly. I wasn't about to wake a guy up just to ask him for a ride. I decided to try my luck on the main drag, and maybe circle back in a while to see if he was awake if no one picked me up.

I started past the truck, then hesitated. Now that I was up closer, something seemed off. I stepped up and stuck my head through the passenger window, making sure I was seeing what I thought I was seeing. His eyes were closed, but his lips were moving, muttering to himself in a low drone. In the jumble of words one jumped out at me: Nevada.

Suddenly the eyes underneath the cap's brim shot open. I jumped, banging my head on the top of the window frame. Without shifting in his seat the man turned his head to look at me, his mouth pulling apart into a stiff smile. When he spoke his voice was low and calm. "May I help you?"

My heart throbbed in time with the back of my head as I considered my next move. The guy was giving me the creeps, and I seriously considered bolting. But the voice in the back of my head reminded me that he sounded like he was going to Nevada, and who knew when my next chance would be? I told myself to calm down. He had probably just been concentrating on plotting out his own journey, a mental-map kind of thing. I was pretty sure I'd heard about something like that on a podcast.

I realized he was still looking at me, the smile still

plastered to his face. He spoke again, and it sounded eerily similar to the first time. "May I help you?"

I smiled back. "You sure can, buddy. I'm heading to Nevada. Any chance I can catch a ride with you?"

"What a coincidence. I am also going to Nevada. Climb in and we will drive together." He quickly put his seat back up and reached over to the passenger door, opening it and smiling expectantly.

I shushed the alarm bells, reminding myself that I wasn't choosy, and tossed my backpack into the truck bed. I noted with amusement that the same exact bag was already in there; he must have stopped at the same place I had. I climbed into the seat next to him as he turned the key, and the engine coughed before rumbling to life. We were immediately blasted by cold air pouring from the vents on the dashboard, which, after the initial shock, was nice.

We pulled out onto the freeway and started moving forward. We were going very slowly, and a few cars laid on their horns as we hugged the slow lane, moving no higher than 45. The few cars out began to pass us, and I sighed as I realized that I had joined up with a cautious driver. *Not choosy, not choosy...*

Rather than moan about it I stuck my hand. "Hey man, thanks for the lift. Name's Randy."

The driver didn't even look at it, his eyes glued to the road in front of us. "My name is...Steven. It is good to meet you."

And that was all he said. We drove in silence for the next fifteen minutes, the only sound a soft static coming from the speakers or the occasional car that passed us. After a bit there were no other cars on the road, and I waited another few minutes before the silence got the better of me.

"Man, I can't believe my luck! I figured I'd have to bum rides with at least a dozen different people on my way up from Long Beach, but here you are. Hey, does this radio work, or do you just like listening to static?"

The only response I got was a slight nod, but I took it as consent and started playing with the knob. It didn't take me long to find a rock station, and after a short news piece about a group of families murdered in Maryland we were jamming out to some Styx. Well, I was.

A few more songs passed, then he switched the radio off right in the middle of some Bowie. Man, I thought, you're the *real* oddity. That made me chuckle a bit.

He waited until I was done before he spoke. "So, Randy. Why are you traveling to Nevada today?"

"That's a funny story actually. You're probably going to think it's stupid, but I'm going to Area 51." I reached down to grab my water bottle out of my bag, then kicked myself for throwing it in the truck bed. This was going to be a long drive.

He sat up straight at that, obviously interested. I smiled. "So I take it you've heard of the whole 'Storm Area 51' thing that everyone's been going on about? Well, I decided screw it, let's go! I mean, I don't believe in aliens or anything like that, but I mean COME ON! How cool would it be to be able to say I was there when everyone mobbed a secret government compound? And everyone's totally alien crazy right now. In fact, I design logos for shirts and I can't tell you how many alien logos I have done in the last few months..."

It took a moment to realize his hand was on my forearm. I looked over at Steven and the hair on the back of my neck began to rise. He was still smiling, but his eyes were weird. They almost looked red in the light coming from the dash. Before I had time to fully process what was going on the hand shot down to my wrist. He flipped my arm over and covered my hand with his.

Every crazy hitchhiker story I had ever heard popped into my mind, and I went into overdrive. I didn't know what freaky stuff this guy was into, but I had no intention of finding out. I pulled up every bit of my training from Big Boy's Peewee Dojo, every move I had mastered, with a mighty yell. Then I realized I had only been there for the introductory class, and promptly dishonored Master Bob and my family by backhanding Steven across the face.

His head snapped back against the car door with a dull thump. He should have been dazed. But the smile remained where it was, and so did his hand.

I felt something starting to tickle my palm, and the panic really set in. I reached out blindly and did the only other thing I could think of. I grabbed the steering wheel, and I gave it a sharp jerk to the right. This time Steven fell back hard against the driver's side window, his hands flying up in surprise. As they did I saw puckered, red sores on the palms of both his hands. All of a sudden my stomach threatened to crowd my lungs.

I forced it back down down with a snarl. It was bad enough this guy was trying to assault me, but he had some sort of *disease* as well?! I was pretty sure that I heard somewhere that that's a felony. I soon realized that we were careening toward the grass on the side of the road, so I threw the wheel back to the left. It brought the truck back on track, but now we were flying down the shoulder of the road. I could feel the grooves marking the edge of the lane shuddering beneath us as I fought to keep us from drifting any further.

I placed my newly-freed hand on Steven's knee and jammed it down, forcing his foot down on the brake pedal. With a squeal the truck lurched against its own weight, and I nearly lost control as we both shot forward against the belts holding us in place. With my jaw clenched I pressed again, a little more steadily this time, and my right hand hovered over the buckle at my hip. I began calculating speeds and angles and distances.

Then I saw Steven reaching out to me again so I bailed out.

I landed hard on the grass, rolling and sliding several feet before finally coming to a stop. I brought my head up just in time to see the truck swing out of control. It swerved onto the road, then back onto the shoulder, tottering before tipping over and rolling. Once, twice, and then it came to a stop on its side.

I struggled to my feet and began to stumble toward it, and got within a hundred feet when I stopped. There, at my feet, was my bag. It must have gotten thrown when the truck began to roll. I stared at it a moment before looking up at the truck, smoking and unmoving. A few cars were already beginning to pull off and stop to see what was going on. I grabbed my bag and started back the way I had come.

As I went I tried to make sense of what had just happened. That was some freaky stuff, and not in the good way. I thought of the couple in the car, then that weirdo trying to do... *something* to me. Was everyone totally insane tonight?

I shook my head. *Must be something in the water.*

PART 4

SEPTEMBER 18, 2019

GERALD

I've learned a lot about cowardice over the years. In particular, I've learned is that there are three distinct levels.

First, there's a base level of cowardice that's defined by primal fear. The "fight or flight" response. If something threatens your physical state of being your mind, and your body, instinctively respond to shield yourself against the threat of violence. You don't have time to think, you just hide, run, cry, or shit your pants.

I've been in this situation, like the time I accidentally forgot to take my iPhone out of my jacket pocket at work. I was supposed to drop it into the cell phone basket right outside the first of three S-4 security gates, but I left it in my pocket. The metal detector clamored when I walked through, and the two guards wielding Marine Corps Issue M16A2's jumped to attention when I reached into my pocket to grab it. They drew their massive guns on me, then they began barking orders I couldn't understand over the machine still going off. Lo and behold, everybody poops.

There's a middle level of cowardice that's defined by regret. You know you're getting fucked, and you know you should do something, but you aren't smart enough or brave enough to think of the right thing to do. I experienced this level when I caught my wife three years into an affair with a State Farm Agent, and she walked out on me because I 'didn't pay enough attention' to her. A stronger man probably would have shown a little backbone, but I'm not a strong man. I just let her walk right over me, then out our front door. Every day since I've wanted that moment back in hopes that I would somehow find the courage just to do something, *anything* about it.

Then there's a third level of cowardice, which is defined by despair. The threat you're facing isn't physical or situational, and it's really quite existential. This deep state of cowardice doesn't come on quick like the first two, instead it's the product of tens of thousands of cowardly micro-decisions over the course of a long period of time. You put yourself into a situation, like my moral job quandaries, and it's like being in a vice-grip. Every day, without you even noticing, the decisions you're blindly making and the asinine orders you're accepting are slowly ticking, cog by cog, tighter and tighter and tighter until you look up one day and you're utterly trapped.

Yesterday my boss asked me to murder a young girl, implant a finger-sized alien named Carl into her brain stem, zip her back up, and start talking to her. A normal person probably would have laughed off the request as insane, profusely protested, or accepted whatever punishment came along with refusal. Me? I croaked out empty air and obeyed. I didn't do anything. I didn't fight it, and I didn't question it. I knew it was wrong, I knew it was the worst thing I'd ever been asked to do by a mile, but I'd been conditioned to be so afraid of everything around me that I wouldn't even know where to start refusing an order.

Whatever moral gumption I had when I first got here had long since been extinguished.

The same could not be said for Carl. After fifty-eight years of captivity and dozens of painful host transitions, Carl, a Tau, a little worm, somehow maintained a moral compass. He and I were discussing mitochondrial evolution, since he had become something of a molecular biologist himself through our conversations, when two guards wheeled the unconscious body of the little girl past the lab and down the hall to the operating room. Carl was currently occupying the body of a rail-thin, middle aged woman who was standing several feet in front of me.

"Gerald. What is that?" Carl snapped, already knowing the answer but making me say it anyway.

I took two steps back from him and sat down on a wheeled stool. The cushion made an audible *PFFTT* when I sat down on it, and Carl glared at me through the eyes of a woman whose facial skin was sagging so much it looked like it was about to melt away. Among his thousands of uncanny abilities when channeling hosts, Carl had a way of throwing the same dark, piercing glare regardless of the eyeballs he was looking through. The glare that was on me now was the same exact glare that had looked right through me when we first met.

"Don't tell me that's what I think it is."

"What, uh, what do you mean?"

"Are you going to put me into that host body?"

I turned around and looked out into the hall, knowing full well the gurney was already gone, but acting like it was still there. "The body that just went through here? Yeah. They want to try it."

"Gerald, I don't know if that's going to work."

"Why not?"

"Is that the body of an undeveloped human?"

"Um, I guess you could say that. Yes."

"Oh. Gerald. No...Gerald! That is not going to work," Carl's tone grew harsher, and his presence felt heavier. He had never physically attacked me before, but I didn't like that we were in the lab together with no walls between us. Over the years he and I had built a level of trust where neither of us believed it to be necessary, but in that instant I almost regretted it.

"Why not, Carl?"

"Because the central nervous system of an immature human is not yet developed. You have witnessed this process dozens of times with your own eyes. You are a skilled and intelligent scientist, and you understand the cause and effect of such a situation."

"Well, I actually don't know what will happen."

"I do, Gerald. Do not do this!"

The talking stopped, and we stared at each other in silence. Carl clenched the bony fingers of his gaunt, female host. My sciatica flared. After a tense moment Carl relaxed his grip, turned around, and ran towards the holding cell. He let out a shriek and slammed his head against the glass wall. His long, wiry, brown hair was waving crazily back and forth. He slammed and slammed and shrieked and slammed, blood rushing down his face, blood splattering on the glass. Within seconds three uniformed guards came in and tackled Carl to the ground.

The shrieks became a loop of, "Kill me! Kill me! Just kill me!" over and over again. One of the guards jammed a tranquilizer syringe in Carl's neck, and the host body went limp. The guards rushed him out of the lab as quickly as they had barged in, and the room was silent again.

I stared at the blood stains on the glass. I hadn't moved from my stool the entire time. I was just sitting there, cowardice my only companion.

Magruder and I stood shoulder-to-shoulder at the edge of the operating room. Carl's current host lay face down on one table, and his new host lay face down on the other. The surgeons and lab techs needed to move fast after what Carl had just done to himself.

"Why her? A child?" I asked calmly. Asking something like 'Where did she come from?' or 'Who is she?' was so far beyond the point now.

"Surely it's not so difficult to understand. The body of a seven-year old human presents us with an unprecedented opportunity to observe how Taus react to an immature body. This is uncharted territory for us, Gerald."

I hated how he always said 'Taus' with a plural, as if there were more than one in captivity, and as if this one didn't have an actual name.

"Are we even sure if the host body can handle this?" I watched as a lab tech sucked Carl up through the baster-looking machine and spit him into a glass beaker. These were the same visuals as all of the other times, but it felt worse.

"Oh, of course not. You'd know better than anybody. What do you think? How do you think the Tau will react?"

A female lab tech drew back the white cover from the small, pale body of the young girl. The lab tech's latex-clad hands gently grasped the girl's hair and parted it down the sides of her face, exposing the back of her neck. She handled it with extreme care, the way a mother might handle her daughter's hair when teaching her how to braid. *Where is THIS girl's mother? Does she know her child is missing? Her baby? Does she know she's unconscious, face down on a steel slab? Surrounded by a half dozen sadistically evil people in lab coats? About to die? Here? In the coldest, darkest place on earth? Does...*

"Gerald, Gerald! Are you listening to me? How do you think she will react?"

A surgeon drew a scalpel, making a clean incision down the back of the girl's delicate neck. I thought about the desperate pleas Carl had made before he attempted to bash his head in. I wasn't sure whether Carl was objecting for physical reasons or moral reasons, but I got the sense that it was a blend of both. A dark streak of blood spilled out and rolled down into the girl's ear, and I had to refrain from retching.

"I, I honestly have no idea, sir."

Another lab tech placed the transition device over the girl's incision. In that moment I wondered if Carl's writhing would just snap the girl's spine, which would put a quick end to this heinousness. In he went, and writhe he did, and from all the way in the back of the room I could see the girl's skin bulge and ripple under Carl's presence. I heard a faint *pop*, and two of the lab techs quickly peered down into the incision. A few minutes later Carl calmed himself, and the surgeon glued and stapled up the incision. The surgical team slowly backed away from the table, and soon they exited the room.

They didn't even cover her up, they just left her there. I couldn't see any emotion through their surgery masks, and these people had to have nerves of the finest steel, but it was clear as day to everyone present that an act of pure evil had just been committed.

A few hours later I was staring at Carl once again, now in the body of a human girl slowly waking up from a nightmare. Carl was on the other side of the glass this time, and I dully noted that the blood had been cleaned up. There was still a cobweb-shaped crack about head height, and the light from the overhead fluorescents glistened off the fragments. It was like a flag of morality planted in the pit of Hell. It was there, even if no one could see it. I noticed a long, triangular piece of glass still on the ground. Something compelled me to walk over, wrap it in a paper towel, and put it in my lab coat pocket.

Just as I bent down I noticed movement out of the corner of my eye. Carl stood up straight, but his head was stuck cocked to the side. That pop I heard might have jostled something in her neck, maybe something around the C-2 area.

"Hey, Carl. How are you feeling?"

Carl let out a deep sigh. He stood up and closed his eyes.

"We didn't know if you were going to make it there. This is very new territory."

Carl opened his eyes and blinked sharply. "Gerald. This host body is undeveloped."

"It is."

Carl patted his chest, his belly, and his legs with his hands. He looked down at his feet. He touched the contours of his face, and winced when his left hand grazed the back of his neck. His head was still cocked.

"I uh, I think you did some damage to the host body there. Are you in a lot of pain?"

"Yes," he seethed, "Gerald..."

I sighed and got up from my stool. I walked over to the edge of the glass and crouched to meet Carl's eyes. I'd never had to crouch to look into his eyes before. He still had a hand on his neck when he said, "So this is one of your young? You put me into one of your young."

"Well, I mean, I personally didn..."

"Shut up. Don't give me that. You disgust me. You all disgust me."

"Can you tell me if C-2 is brok..."

"What's new about this? What are you learning here? You took an undeveloped body and you broke it by shoving me inside. It's broken, Gerald. And you broke it."

I didn't know whether that was a confirmation that C-2 was broken, or if the barb had some higher meaning. Carl had a tendency to be vitriolic when first entering a new host body, but this was a new level of intensity. It could have been the pain talking, but he also could have been trying to tap into a new level of guilt within me that was clearly exposed.

"You took an undeveloped body and broke it. You took an undeveloped body and broke it Gerald!"

"Carl, I..."

"Stop." He blinked his eyes twice and looked up at the ceiling. "Gerald..." Carl slowly sat down, crossed his legs, and began breathing heavily. He suddenly didn't look well.

I stood up. "Carl? Are you okay?"

Carl's breathing became heavier. "Gerald...you...
I...hate...look what you've...done to..."

His eyes rolled skywards, his torso crumpled, and
the back of his head made a *thunk* when it smacked
into the cold floor. The head of a little girl.

I woke up just before noon on Tuesday, and everything from my neck down hurt like Hell. The previous evening ran through my mind like a bad movie, and I mentally cringed.

After grabbing my bag I had run for a good mile or so, When I finally stopped, hunched and coughing, I realized I should probably call someone to come get me. My parents were out of town, but maybe I could get my buddy Phil to drive out. I pulled out my phone to call him, and that's how I discovered I had landed on my phone when I bailed out of the truck. I sighed, sticking out my thumb.. I'd just have to settle for a shower, and some sleep.

I know, hitchhiking sounds stupid after what had

just happened, but what were the odds that I'd get picked up by two weirdos in a row?

It took a while for someone to stop. I don't blame them, since I probably wouldn't have stopped for a beat-up, muddy guy clutching a backpack either. Finally a couple pulled over, and I climbed into their backseat next to a sleeping baby. I spent the whole ride to the nearest motel holding my breath, and I barely spoke. I'd put up with a lot, but screaming babies? If I'd wanted to deal with that I would have flown to Nevada.

I walked into the motel office and asked for a room, but didn't get the best reaction from the desk clerk. The girl behind the counter looked me up and down, rolled her eyes, and popped her gum before pushing a key over the counter. Well, at least I still had my wallet.

The room was dark and dingy, about what I expected from that type of place. The wallpaper looked like it had been put up in the seventies, and it was starting to peel. The lone bed, which they dubiously called a queen, was pushed against the wall across from a table with a small flat screen TV on it. I flopped down on the bed and grabbed the remote, figuring I could switch it on to see if there was anything good to watch, or at least if it had anything other than the local public stations.

My stomach chose that moment to make itself known. I realized I hadn't eaten since having a snack at that rest stop. I dropped the remote next to me and reached across the bed for my backpack. When I woke up my fingers were still curled around the strap.

I slowly pulled myself out of bed, my body complaining every inch of the way. I waddled into the bathroom and caught a look at myself in the mirror, and it wasn't a pretty sight. My blonde hair was a dusty tan, and I could see a bruise formed underneath my sleeve crawling up my thin shoulder. I took a piss, then stood there a moment decide whether to grab a bite to eat or take a shower.

My stomach finally made that decision for me.

I had packed trail mix and power bars in my bag, since I had planned for a long stretch of uncertainty. But at that moment, all I wanted was chocolate. I had grabbed a few bags of Reese's Pieces at the check stand (it seemed appropriate), and they were calling my name. I walked back out and unzipped my bag.

It wasn't my bag.

I swore under my breath. I must have grabbed that

Steven guy's bag by mistake. This one was full of clothes, but none of them were mine. I pulled out an ugly plaid shirt and winced; then I realized something even worse. It actually looked like it might fit me. I didn't have anything to wear except the muddy, torn outfit I'd left town with, so I sighed and started pulling out the bag's contents to see if there was anything better. After what the guy had put me through he owed me something, even if it was just bad fashion sense.

I pulled out a pair of cargo shorts, and there it was. A long, metal cylinder, about the size of a thermos but slightly thicker. It must have been made of stainless steel or something, since the surface was shiny and I could almost make my face out in the reflection. Damn, I still needed to shower.

First, however, I wanted to see what was inside. There was a tiny crack near what I assumed was the top of it, so I tried to twist it off. I gripped it and turned, but nothing happened. I tried pushing down and turning. Still nothing. Finally I gave up and tossed it back into the bag. It landed upside down, and I noticed a small panel on the bottom. It was clear and underneath it, set back into the cylinder, was a button. I decided to check it out after taking that hot shower. All that physical labor had woken my muscles up, and they were cranky.

Ten minutes later I climbed out of the shower and grabbed a towel. My body wasn't happy yet, but at least it had calmed down a bit.

I was drying my arms when I heard it. Someone was jiggling the knob of the door to my room. I wondered why someone would be trying to get in... I was pretty sure I had hung the Do Not Disturb sign on the door as soon as I had gotten there, and I heard somewhere that bothering someone while the sign was there is enough to get you fired. I was about to call out to tell housekeeping to come back later, but before I could the door popped open. And the voices that came through didn't sound like any maids I had ever met.

"...cannot believe she decided to put Steven in charge of something so imperative. Thank goodness for the tracking system we put on it."

My blood ran cold as the words sunk in. Steven? As in the creep from last night? All of a sudden I wished I *had* flown to Nevada. I quickly flicked the light switch down, plunging the bathroom into darkness.

From the sound of it there were two men out there. They passed by where I stood, and I was struggling to control my breathing so it wouldn't be heard. I could hear their feet clomping towards the bed, as well as a crinkling noise. It sounded like paper, or some sort of thin plastic.

"We will have a talk with her about it when we all meet up at the gate. For now, the mission is to retrieve the unit and transport it to the end of the road. Check the bag."

I heard the creak of the bedsprings as one of them sat down. "It is still here. Gather up all of these things and return them to the bag. We must leave no traces of our visit."

This was followed by a series of shuffling sounds before the bag was zipped closed, and as they finished I heard the crinkling resume.

"Have you tried these? They are quite good."

"Come on, we must get out of here. This must be at the gate when the time is right. I hope we will not have to use it, but it is good to have a second plan in place."

They walked back past me and out the door.

Very slowly I eased the bathroom door open and peered out, and thankfully the room was empty. So was the bed; the bag was gone.

I plopped down on the bed, my mind reeling. What had just happened? My room had been invaded by two guys, and they were looking for the bag I had accidentally taken from the guy I had caught a ride with the night before. I thought about the canister tucked underneath everything, and suddenly it hit me. There was only one explanation.

Drugs.

I had somehow stumbled into some drug mule operation. That's why Steven had been so sick, and why he'd been acting so weird. My heart dropped as my mind conjured up images of what might have happened if I had been discovered, and I really wished I still had my phone. No way was Phil going to believe this!

I tossed the towel on the bed and reached for...

Great. They had taken the clothes along with everything else when they took the bag. Sighing, I bent down to collect my muddy pants. As I did something caught my eye.

In the trash can in the corner was something that had not been there when I went to take my shower. I carefully took it out. It was a candy wrapper. My teeth clenched as I realized that not only did they have Steven's bag now, they also had mine.

And those bastards were eating my Reese's Pieces!

CARRIE

7:55 P.M.

So far I had counted to ten thirty-four times. That was three-hundred-and-forty eyes, one-hundred-and-seventy-two people. I had begun counting as people started walking into the meeting space, as they sat down and chatted with their friends. I kept counting as Craig started the meeting, introducing himself and the rest of the Truth Bringers, while I awkwardly stood and waved at the group of onlookers around us. We had scattered ourselves throughout the audience, placing ourselves throughout the group so that we could answer any questions that might come up during the meeting.

This was probably the most difficult part for me, being so close to so many people as their hot breath mingled with mine. Accidental brushes against my shoulder when the person beside me shifted, or the way the little girl behind me kept tapping her foot against the picnic table I was seated on, were enough to put my anxiety on edge. I could feel my heart pounding in my ears, and I struggled to maintain control as I heard Craig wrapping up his talk on the history of Area 51 and the secrets the government had been conspiring to keep from us.

It was almost time.

One... two... three... four... five... six... seven... eight...nine... ten...

I clenched my hand until my nails bit into my flesh, the sharp pain of breaking skin calming me as it snapped me back to reality.

It was different during the day when I was handing out flyers and talking to people. Although I was hot, and uncomfortable, I still had control. Just like driving on a busy highway, I could always look ahead to make sure that I left enough space between us that I could make a quick exit if need be, but there were no exits on this picnic table. A group of Unbelievers had set a blanket on the ground below me, blocking any escape route. Hot, sweaty bodies were seated beside me and directly behind me, and I felt trapped.

"Now I would like to turn the meeting over to

Carrie Lane, our Truth Bringer, all the way from Nome, Alaska. You may already know her from around the gates handing out flyers and chatting with you about why we are here, but did you know it was *her* encounter story featured on those same flyers?" Craig waved his arm towards me, signaling it was my turn to stand. "Give it up for Carrie, who has the courage to share her story and spread the truth here today."

I stood, a wide smile plastered on my face. Small droplets of blood dripped down my palm.

One...two...three...four...five...six...seven...eight...

We had talked about these meetings for months. What we would say, who would share their stories and experiences, how to answer questions. At the time I had no issue with it, but that was before I saw all these faces staring at me. That was before I had spent days in the unending heat until my head was heavy and my vision blurred, and days before I had punched the asshole Drone in the face and had to be hauled back to base camp.

...eight..nine..ten...

"Hi. My name is Carrie Lane, and I was abducted when I was five years old." Shit, I was talking as if this was a freaking Aliens Abduction Support group meeting. I cleared my throat, sweat beginning to accumulate on my forehead as I struggled to remember what I was going to say.

A gloved hand handed me a bottle of clear liquid and I drank it quickly, draining the bottle before realizing it wasn't water. The liquid burned going down, like the cheap moonshine my uncle used to make, and hit my empty stomach hard. I stifled a cough, my head already beginning to spin.

"Hi, sorry about that," I said, gaining liquid courage, and I began to smile. *I can do this.* "Some of you have already met me, walking the gates alongside you, handing you the same flyer you are holding right now. Months ago, when the original Facebook event was created, I was lucky enough to find this group of wonderful people that you see before you. Together we found comradery, and we discovered that most of the population had been brainwashed into believing lies," I looked around the open space, three-hundred-and-forty eyes staring back at me intently. More clear bottles like the one I had just drank were being passed around, and the group and drank readily.

I continued, my voice loud and clear now. "The government has spent hundreds of millions of dollars protecting this lie, and has conspired for decades to keep you in the dark about it. But the truth is simple:

everything you have ever been told is a lie. The truth is HERE, and so are the aliens!"

Someone cheered from across the space, and soon others followed. A small applause fanned around the circle as I continued.

"When I was five years old I was taken from my father's hunting shack outside of Nome, Alaska during a family hunting trip. For four days I was poked and prodded, used and abused like I was nothing. Like I was worthless, not even human, like I was something to be experimented on." A stray tear escaped my eye, but I refused to wipe it away. Let them see it. "The search and rescue team found me abandoned miles away from the cabin, frostbitten and near death. My injuries so extensive it took multiple surgeries and months of recovery, leaving my family not only with a broken child, but a horrible financial burden they couldn't afford.

The police assumed I was kidnapped by a vagrant, a person passing through that happened upon me, but that wasn't true. When I tried to tell them about the creatures that did this to me they laughed at me. Five-year-old me, barely able to breathe, and they just laughed. They told me I had made it all up, and said that I just wanted attention. But I didn't want any attention. I didn't want any of what happened to me. Doctors, therapists, even my own family didn't believe me. No one believed me. For years they told me I had made it up, and over and over again I was told I had imagined it."

I was yelling now, my voice booming around me, but the crowd gathered around me didn't care. They were all listening intently, their bodies bent towards me, eagerly awaiting what else I had to say. I smiled. For the first time in as long as I could remember people were not only listening to me, but believing me.

"For years I was told that my memories weren't real, but I can tell you what is real." I lifted my shirt up, exposing three thick scars along my abdomen, gnarled and tender even after so long. The crowd gasped. I could see their eyes look away, and then back with a grotesque curiosity. They wanted more. "This is real. These scars are real, and the aliens that gave them to me are real as well. That is what your government is protecting you from."

I screamed, pointing towards the gate beyond the trailers. They all turned and followed my finger, engrossed in my words. "That's why we're here! We're here to demand answers!" I pounded my fist into my bleeding hand. "We're here to demand an end to the charade, an end to the lies and deception.

If they have nothing to hide then they should LET US IN!"

I looked over at Craig across the meeting space, and I was glad his smile was wide and his eyes were bright. He nodded towards me, clearly a *Job well done* nod. I had convinced them. I had convinced them all, and they would follow us through even Hell's gates at this point.

"The truth is here, beyond those gates, and in two days we're going to get it!"

The crowd roared with me. They stood and rushed towards me, grabbing my arms and hoisting me above their heads. They carried me as they chanted, and I felt the hot tears of joy streaming down my face. I had done it.

"THE TRUTH IS HERE! THE TRUTH IS HERE!"

PART 5

SEPTEMBER 19, 2019

LOGAN

If I could go back in time, I'd bitchslap myself right before I volunteered to tend bar at Area 51.

Someone on the Facebook group put out the call for people who would be willing to mix and hand out drinks to all the people who were gathering for the raid, and like an idiot I'd agreed. I had a few years of bartending experience under my belt that had helped put me through college, so it made sense that I would be one of the ones who offered my services. Plus, it was a potential thousands of people who might tip for their alcohol.

Well, it turned out to be nothing like I had pictured. I thought maybe they'd have a nice little cantina setup with tables and chairs and those string lights to give it some atmosphere. That would have been nice. In reality it was thousands of sweaty, rowdy people crammed underneath giant white tents demanding booze faster than we could pour it. I was stationed behind a row of fold-out tables that separated us from row after row of chairs, and it gave me the vibe of one of those old-time revival tents. Praise be the almighty plastic cup! But none of us were having any transcendent experiences, especially at these prices. $12.50 for a jack and coke? No wonder no one was leaving tips.

Take the guy closest to me. He'd been hunched in his chair for an hour and a half, downing vodka and cranberry one after the other. Beyond the exuberant bill, which he didn't seem to care about, I took immediate notice of him because of how he was dressed. In the midst of a crowd in t-shirts and shorts he sat in a white, button-up dress shirt and a lab coat. If I didn't know any better I'd say he was a super-secret scientist, and he even had a badge sticking out of his front pocket. I tried to get a look at it while pouring drinks, but I couldn't make out any recognizable details beyond a scan code.

I don't know what his deal was, but he was obviously in a bad way. In all my years as a bartender I've seen enough to know when someone's hit rock bottom, and this guy showed all the signs. Messy hair, untucked shirt, eyes somehow equally zoned out and hyper focused. I had tried to engage him when I brought him his first drink, but he just stared at me vacantly and muttered, "I can't talk about it."

Not that I had a lot of time to socialize with anyone anyway. I was one of five people taking care of drinks for this crazy mob. We had most of your basic liquors, all of them rail drinks, super cheap and grossly overpriced. Then we had some standard mixers, and ten kegs of cheap beer. I was happy whenever anyone ordered a cup of brew since it gave me a chance to take a breath, pour, and watch everyone for a moment.

About five vodka cranberries in, Lab Coat was joined by another man. This guy was short and had tousled blond hair, like he hadn't brushed it in days. I couldn't decide if it was a look, or if he actually hadn't brushed it. What really grabbed me was his shirt though. It was the same exact shirt all those crazy alien lovers were wearing, "The truth is out there" or something like that, but his was two sizes too small. It was riding up and exposing his midriff, but he was grinning away like it was the coolest thing he'd ever seen. He kept looking down at it and running his fingers over the logo on it.

He looked up after a few minutes of admiring his

shirt and walked through the crowd, nodding to fellow t-shirt wearers. He asked for a beer, and as I poured it for him he pointed excitedly at the shirt and practically shouted, "I made this!"

He must have noticed me looking further down to where it rode up his middle, because he followed it up with, "They only had women's left!" before grabbing the cup from me and taking a swig.

It finally hit me what he reminded me of: a Hobbit! Small little dude, drinking a huge beer, super excited about everything. This guy was definitely a Hobbit.

I chuckled a bit, glancing around the room while I poured the next round of drinks that came in. The tent was buzzing with all types of drinkers tonight. Couples drinking in pairs, groups mingling between the chairs or dancing in the corner to the sounds coming from the party tent down the road. Then there were the single drinkers, silently sipping their booze in the corners.

Not for the first time my eyes drifted to the left side of the tent to where a tall woman with dark, auburn hair clutched a rum and Coke. Her curvy body was wrapped in a long black trench coat, which I found odd because it was still hot as hell outside, even with the sun setting. Upon arrival she had pushed her way through the crowd amidst protests and shouts, looked me in the eye, and said, "Rum and coke. Now." I thought it wise to just do as she said.

She had been here for a while now, just watching everyone while she occasionally scribbled something on her notepad. Though she was easy on the eyes she was giving me an uneasy feeling, like I wouldn't want to meet her in a back alley. Every so often she'd get up, walk over to someone, stick out her hand and then not shake theirs when they returned the gesture. She'd stare at the other person's hand for a second, then walk back to her spot without a word. She'd brood for a while before scanning the room again, and the process would repeat.

She seemed especially interested in the crew with black gloves. There were quite a few of them around, and they had been coming in and out all day with different people. They must have been some sort of club or something, since almost all of them wore the same kind of t-shirt that Hobbit was sporting, and they all ordered the exact same drink: beer mixed with soda water. Never in my life had I poured that for anyone, and now I had a bunch of people all asking for it at once. I almost poured a cup for myself, convinced that they knew something I didn't, but I refrained. I just couldn't see how that could work, and it seemed like a waste of good beer. I might have thought the whole thing was weird if I wasn't serving drinks to Lab Coat, Hobbit, Scary-Hot Chick and thousands of other people who looked like they had stepped out of a comic book under a tent in the Nevada desert.

I didn't get the gloves though. That's the *last* thing I would have chosen to wear in the desert, especially black ones. Their palms must have been super sweaty, maybe even cracked or blistering, but they kept them on the entire time. They mainly talked amongst themselves, and drank their weird beer-sodas.

Lab Coat waved me over, and I poured him another refill. I decided I'd have to cut him off soon; he was pretty far gone. "Shit man, almost outta cranberry!" I said, trying to be funny. He didn't even acknowledge me, just kept talking to Hobbit. The two of them seemed to be hitting it off, so the vodka must have been loosening his tongue a bit.

I caught a bit of their conversation as I set his drink down in front of him. As sloshed as he was, Lab Coat still seemed to be choosing his words carefully. "...can't take this anymore. I don't agree with anything we're doing, but I just don't know what to do. I have to do... something...but if I don't do anything..."

Hobbit shook his head. "That's rough, buddy. And you look like you haven't slept in a while. I heard somewhere that work stress is one of the leading causes of sleep loss. If hitchhiking across America has taught me anything, it's that..."

I turned back to the table, and that's when I saw a newcomer walk in. She slowly pushed her way through the outer crowd and stood silently at the back of the waiting mass. I looked her over, and of all the people I'd served that day she was the one who most looked like she needed a drink. She looked downtrodden, as if someone had just told her that her dog had contracted some rare form of canine cancer. I kept an eye on her as I served the rest of the crowd, waiting for her to finally get to the table.

Her order was simple. "Gin and tonic, please. Make it a double."

Rather than pour it immediately I took a moment, my tone gentle. "Hey, are you alright? Can I help you with anything?"

She looked at me, her dark brown eyes worn and exhausted. I could tell she had no more tears left to shed, at least not sober ones. "I lost my son," Her voice was soft as she pulled out her phone, swiping through picture after picture until she settled on a family photo. It looked like they were at the beach, and were happy. An older couple, their hair greying, sat in the sand alongside two teenagers with fire engine red hair. There was also a small boy, maybe two or three, with blond hair and a toothy smile. "Have you seen anyone in this picture? Or just the little boy? His name is Trevor, at least it was... he might be here with his dad Greg."

I took the phone, making sure to zoom in and look at all the faces, but I hadn't seen any of them in the last few days. I shook my head, passing it back to her as her face fell even further. I've done my fair share of playing shrink behind the bar, listening to a lot of sad stories, but some come out of the blue and just sucker punch you. There were no words that could make the situation any better, so instead I poured her a drink, looked her in the eye, and said, from the bottom of my heart, "I'm so sorry."

She nodded slightly, grabbing the cup from me and then easing back into the crowd. I tried to keep an eye on her as she went, but I lost her pretty quickly. I did notice that the Glove Posse were leaving though. They walked side by side, and as they went I realized their steps were in sync.

I put another tick in the secret society column.

As I was moving to the other end of the bar another movement caught my eye. Scary-Hot Chick had gotten up, and she was shoving her way through the crowd. Her eyes were pinned to the tent pole that the Gloves had just walked past on their way out. She had pulled her cell phone out, and was putting it up to her determined face. I watched her leave, and would have spent a little more time speculating if a fresh wave of demanding bodies hadn't chosen that moment to push forward for another round.

None of the orders were very complicated, and I served them pretty quickly, all things considered. A lot of beers, a few straight liquors, and I even had time to talk to a security guy hired by one of the dance party vendors about the group patrolling the gate. He had some very interesting ideas about what they really were, and about who was actually paying them to keep the facility safe from the protesters. I humored him and smiled when he slipped a few bills into my palm. Who am I to disagree with a conspiracy theory?

Suddenly Lab Coat shot up. He clapped Hobbit on the shoulder, then grasped it to steady himself as he tottered a bit. When he was finally standing relatively straight he proclaimed, in a voice much louder than he thought it was, "You're right! All this time I've been trying to make everyone else, like that pompous ass Magruder, everyone else happy. But *screw* Magruder! Screw him right in his big dumb face. I... *am* my own man. And I *do* deserve to be... happy. I'm going to go save that little girl Carl!"

With those final, puzzling words he stumbled out into the sunshine, coat billowing behind him. Hobbit strode up to my table and beamed. "Well, guess that takes care of that. He just needed a push in the right direction. Though I wonder who named that poor girl Carl..."

I smiled as I poured him another beer. "Nice job. Careful though, or you might just put me out of business."

As he opened his mouth to reply there was a commotion at the back of the tent. I sighed and closed my eyes and quietly sighed when I saw what it was. The Crazies had arrived. Again. Every night after their meeting they came in to harass the drunks. And right in the lead was Queen Crazy. She didn't waste any time before she started in on the nearest person, shoving a flyer into his chest and babbling about the government. He tried to get away, but she just followed him for several steps before turning and grabbing the next poor soul.

Hobbit nodded his head at them and asked, "Who's that?"

"That, my good man, is the Abduction Crew. They all think they've been taken and probed in unspeakable places, and that the government is covering it all up. They're determined to tell everyone else their crazy stories, and maybe indoctrinate them into their cult. I'm not excited to see what they plan to do tomorrow."

He laughed and slammed his cup on the table. A bit of beer sloshed out and onto his hand, and he quickly sucked it up. He leaned across the makeshift bar towards me, and he didn't seem to notice as I leaned away. "Oh, I know all about that. You could say alien hysteria runs in my family."

He leaned in closer, making sure I could hear what he had to say next. "You see, my mom's grand-father ran off back in the day, but Nana could never accept that. She lived around here, so of course she told herself that he was taken by the little green men. Or little grey men, as she said. Hey, did I tell you that I once..."

He just kept talking, oblivious to the growing space between us as I stepped away to wipe the tabletop and serve the next customer. I was surprised to discover that there wasn't anyone in front of me.

The tent was pretty empty except for Hobbit, Sad Lady, the Crazies, and a handful of other people determined to finish their drinks. I guess that was one good thing about the Crazies: when they showed up everyone else suddenly discovered they had somewhere else to be and vanished, which gave me a chance to take a breather.

I glanced back at Hobbit and nodded to let him know I was still listening, and he forged ahead. "...so Phil says, *I don't care if she's the pope, she can't come in here dripping all over my carpet...*"

I held my breath as Queen Crazy approached Sad Lady. They briefly shook hands, and Queen handed her a flyer and began talking as she turned it over in her hands. I subtly moved closer, ready to intervene if those nuts thought they could harass a poor, grieving woman. I moved towards the end of the row of tables, wiping as I went so I could hear what they were saying.

Queen was going on like the place really was a revival. "They don't want us to know the truth, and they want to deny us our God-given right to know the world around us and what's really going on. What they don't want us to know is this: we're not alone. The aliens are here, and they're behind that gate."

She paused and stared at the woman seated in front of her, her eyes sharp as she waited for a response. And I think the Queen may have been even more surprised than I was when she heard the words that came out of Sad Lady's mouth.

"I know."

In that moment the tent seemed to fall completely silent. All the Crazies stopped their speeches and raised their heads, all eyes on the one woman who had stopped the world with two words. Finally Queen spoke, her voice a reverent hush. "What did you say?"

Sad Lady raised her head. "I know. They took my son."

Queen Crazy stared at her for a moment longer, then threw her arms around her in an unexpected hug. In all the times I'd seen her, Queen had never physically touched anyone. They stayed like that for a minute, just holding each other in silence. Then Queen pulled away, grabbed Sad Lady's arm, and pulled her to her feet. The two walked out of the tent towards the Crazies' camp, heads close together like they were sharing secrets.

I sat back on one of the empty chairs next to Hobbit, shaking my head. Pulling a napkin out of my pocket I swiped it across my forehead, shaking my head in surprise. The heat was bringing out all kinds of weirdos I guess.

As if he had read my mind Hobbit turned, smiling happily at me. "How's this for a shirt design? Aliens crash-land in a forest. The caption is 'Take me to your cedar'!"

It might have just been the heat, but that did make me chuckle.

PART 6

The shuttle of gloom bumped and clunked its way back to Site S-4. With my hand in the pocket of my lab coat I rubbed my thumb across the flat side of the piece of glass, the one that had come loose when Carl threw his fit of martyrdom. I had forgotten it was still there, and security hadn't flagged it because it wasn't metal. I never understood that security loophole. There was so much I didn't understand.

I couldn't get the events of two days ago out of my head. Carl's fit, his plea for death, the little girl's body face-down on the slab, Carl channeling his anger through her tiny face. I had heard somewhere that the most dangerous man was one with nothing to lose, and while I didn't have much experience being dangerous I did have a lot of practice losing things.

I had finally hit my breaking point, and I wanted to burn this place to the fucking ground.

I strode with confidence through the security checkpoints, three in all between the bus drop-off and the lab. I looked at the faces of everyone who occupied a position on my path. My *warpath*. The bus driver, my colleagues on the bus, the guards. They were all complicit, and they all facilitated the evil that went down in this pit of Hell. The sense of utter freedom I felt in this moment was immense, and I didn't care anymore. I didn't care! It was as if Gerald had died and a new man was reborn. I was a man on a mission.

Carl was sitting on the floor of the holding cell when I got there. His head was slumped forward in fatigue, sadness, or both. I opened the holding cell door, slipped in, closed it behind me, and crouched down to face him. I leaned in and rested my elbows on my knees.

"Carl. Hey..." I did my best to stay quiet. I had no idea to what degree this place was bugged, but it felt safe inside the closed quarters of the holding cell. I nudged his shoulder when he didn't respond.

He struggled to lift his head, and I'm sure it felt

like it weighed a hundred pounds. He sighed, but said nothing.

"Carl, listen. Listen to me! I want to get you out of here. I want to help you."

This information didn't register. The idea of escape or release had become unfathomable to him decades ago. "Gerald. Help me up, please."

I grabbed him under his arms and lifted him up off the ground, the body feather-light.

He struggled to stand as his eyes drifted open and shut. "I need to get out of this body, Gerald. This body... is..."

"I know. It's undeveloped. I know, Carl. I'm sorry. We made a mistake. *I* made a mistake. *I* did, I fucked up. I've been fucking up for the last fourteen years. We've been fucking up ever since we found you." I was manic now, ready to confess all my sins, and to atone for all the evil I had done. "But no more. I want to help you leave. Could you fly your ship if I got you to it?"

"My ship? Gerald. I ...can't fly it. It requires ...the body of what you call a Grey."

"Really? You can't fly it with this body? I thought maybe it would be small enough."

"The size is not the problem. It is the metaphysical connection...this body, your bodies wouldn't work. If there was…" Carl's eyes closed and his knees buckled.

"Shit. Carl! Hey!" I caught the small body and eased it to the ground. "Hey. Are you with me? Can you hear me?"

"Yes." He kept his eyes closed and took deep breaths.

"You were saying something about the ship. If you had what? Do you remember?"

He took a moment to respond, almost as if he couldn't quite remember what we were talking about. "Yes. This…there would need to be a ship specifically…for this host."

"Okay, so that's out. What do you want to do?"

"This host cannot maintain me. I want to die, Gerald."

"Fuck! No. I…Carl, snap out of it buddy. You've made it this far! For years you have made my life miserable, fighting tooth and nail for every test, every procedure, every step along the way. They've held you captive and murdered your kind, yet you remain. You're still here Carl, and that isn't by chance. You're a fighter. You aren't allowed to sit back and die right at the finish line." I gazed into the soft, brown eyes of the little girl, her small frame broken beneath my hands. "Carl. You're a leader, the Tau still need you."

He lifted his head, his back straightening in the small body as resolve and determination seemed to awaken his spirit.

"You are right. There is no more time... I must get out. I have been here too long."

"Yes. Okay, so how could we get you out?"

"I don't know. But... there are other Taus out there. I can... if you get me to them."

"So what? Just get you outside?"

"I need to get out of this body. And then, yes, just get me outside, out of this facility. Somewhere safe. I will contact them."

"Okay. Okay, and I'll help you. I'm going to help you, Carl. We're going to get you out of here and we're going to get you home."

I got to work. I scooped up Carl's body in my arms and placed him on a rolling gurney in the corner of the lab. I covered him in a white sheet, and I rolled him through the hall as though it was the most natural thing ever. If anyone asked what I was doing I could just say we were doing some blood tests, which was a thing that I'd done hundreds of times before with him. I handcuffed his hand to the metal guard rail just for normalcy, and we progressed steadily down the hallways.

Everything to this point had been risky, but not

crazy. What I was about to do was fucking insane. I worked quickly, not only to minimize my chance of getting caught but also because I didn't know how long this new, brave Gerald would last. We made it to one of the operating rooms, and I made sure we were alone.

I flipped the small body over, silently apologizing to the girl it once was, and snatched the baster-looking instrument. I didn't know exactly how it worked, but I had seen it used so many times that I had faith I could figure it out. The neck wound from the previous operation hadn't quite healed, so after reopening it I held the device in place right above the incision.

"Okay. Hold still buddy, I'm coming in," I flicked the switch and pressed the activation button.

SHOOMPFH

It worked. I had him in the device, his small body squirming in the glass tube. He wouldn't be comfortable, but I knew he could survive in the small canister for at least a few hours. Just as I tucked the device into my lab coat pocket and out of sight I heard someone walking down the hall towards us. *Shit*. I picked up the empty host body and gently placed her back onto my rolling gurney. "I'm so sorry, sweetie," I said as I covered the body back up.

We needed a new host body. *Now*.

"Gerald, are you in here?"

A smile slowly crept across my face as Magruder walked into the room, confusion evident in the way he wrinkled his eyebrows.

"Gerald, what's going on here?"

"We've got a problem. Come on, I'll show you in the lab."

I wheeled and walked, moving as fast as I could to avoid questions. Magruder scurried behind me.

"What's the problem? Did the transition fail?"

"Yes, it did. But I have an idea," I moved around, trying to make myself look busy. "I want to revive this host and test its motor functions."

That shut him up. At the end of the day, he had no goddamned idea what he was talking about. Not the way I did. Back in the lab I scooped the little girl up, placing her corpse in the holding cell.

"Magruder, take a look at the incision. The abrasions are alarming, so I'm going to try and disinfect this wound."

Magruder got down on his knees and cupped the girl's head in his hands. I locked my eyes on the back of his head, my adrenaline soaring as I stood there watching him. I batted away my first level of cowardice, grabbed the hair on the back of his head, and blasted his forehead against the wall. I let go and he buckled to the floor, out cold.

I had to take a moment to savor this sight. "Hooo boy. Whoa boy..."

Then I got to work before I could hyperventilate. I had everything I needed right there in the holding cell, so I pulled the suction device from my pocket and placed it on the ground.

Carl was wiggling one side of his body, a silent decree of "I'm still alive!"

I kneeled over Magruder's body and pulled down his shirt collar, exposing the back of his neck. From my other pocket I withdrew the piece of glass, the one that had come off the wall during Carl's fit. Before I sliced into Magruder's flesh I shot a look over my shoulder at the web of broken glass still on the wall of the cell. "Well done, buddy," I said quietly.

I drove the sharpest end into Magruder's neck with immense pleasure, and drew the glass in a downward motion. Once I had a big enough incision to work with I tossed the glass shard aside, and I grabbed the suction instrument. I positioned it, put the switch in reverse, then flicked it on.

FOOOMMPPH.

Carl was in.

I held Magruder's lifeless body in my arms. I looked at my watch, and it was 9:22 a.m. Carl needed about four hours to worm into the CNS and bring his new host to life, and I had no damn idea what to do with Magruder's body until then. Would anyone come looking for him? Did he even work with anyone? I had never met, or even heard of, his boss, but I also knew he didn't run this place. Besides, there really was no good place to hide him in the lab. Everything was one big open room, and the holding cell walls were glass so if someone walked in they'd see him. For a second I entertained the idea of trying to stand him up like a mannequin, but I settled on placing his body on the gurney like I did with the little girl and covering him with a sheet. It was the least shitty option I had.

Once that was complete I wheeled the gurney into a corner of the room and checked my watch. He had only been twelve minutes. *Christ, this is going to be the longest four hours of my life.*

The girl's body was less of a problem, but the inside the holding cell was a mess and I needed something to do, so I decided to start cleaning. The amount of blood this whole thing had caused was kind of incredible. A proper surgeon wouldn't have made nearly such a mess. As it was there was blood all over the floor of the cell, all over my lab coat (*Shit, how am I going to explain THAT?*) and *oh fuck!* I was traipsing around the lab, leaving bloody footprints.

The first order of business became scrubbing my bloody footprints off the floor of the lab. I slipped off my shoes and placed them in the utility sink by the far wall, which also had cabinets containing cleaning supplies. I retraced my steps and erased my bloody tracks easily enough, but the holding cell was a tougher job. The blood had pooled enough to create a watermelon-sized puddle of crimson, and blood really enjoys smearing. Once the holding cell was clean I picked up the little girl's body, leaning in the corner as though she was sitting up.

I didn't know what else to do with her, and on impulse I kissed her on the forehead as I readied myself to leave the confines of this place for the very last time.

ELAIN

11:32 A.M.

The bustling road that leads from the Extraterrestrial Highway all the way to the gate was filled with people, and they had turned the fun festival of meandering party-goers to full on Burning Man overnight. The already-overcrowded desert was swarming with newly-arrived partygoers and tourists with their phones at the ready, looking for the perfect Instagram photo complete with alien filter. I watched from my rented Toyota Matrix, crouched in the backseat trying to will away the gin headache, when the busses had begun to arrive first thing in the morning. Droves of unsuspecting people, eager and excited to take part in what they expected to be the event of the century, had tumbled out of the bus after bus into the hot, oven-like desert.

I wondered briefly if anyone had told them about the conditions on the ground at the gate. It was a long walk from the highway, and there weren't many places to stop for refreshments. The night before I couldn't help but notice the mounting tensions between the two sides. The soldiers had positioned themselves in full riot gear in front of the gates, their bodies a barrier between the clashing crowds and the government facility. Beyond them armoured trucks and tanks had been stationed within view of the gates, an ever-present threat of force to those challenging authority.

A line in the sand had been drawn. One side had deemed themselves the "Protectors", a group of extremists armed and ready to fight to protect the government at all cost. They saw this raid as an attack on America herself. A war. On the other side there were the "Truth Bringers". Both groups were armed with conviction and bodies. Not to mention guns, lots and lots of guns. It boggles my mind how in this particular state you were allowed to carry weapons in the open, where were they getting them all from? Security and police had their hands full trying to keep the groups from crossing over into the other group's territory, but I doubted that would last long if what Carrie had said last night in the bar was true. They were planning on forcing their way through, and they were going to expose the government's lies.

If anyone had any sense they wouldn't be anywhere near the gates when it happened.

I packed the last of my water in a small backpack and slung it over my shoulder, catching a glimpse of myself in the reflection of the car window. I looked rough. I had cleaned myself up a bit since the police station incident, stopping at a gas station restroom on the way to the car rental place. I had picked up a new shirt and disposed of the blood-soaked one from the night before, and I had even given myself a bath with a wet paper towel in the small bathroom sink. I rinsed my hair clean of blood, and I scrubbed my hands until they were raw, but that had been two days ago. The sweat and dust of the desert had since taken over, coating me in a brown film. Streaks of clean skin were visible against the caked-on dirt where my tears had washed it away, but that was as clean as I got.

I grabbed a dirty take-out napkin and scrubbed my face as best as I could. My hair was mass of tangles, so using my fingers and a pen I found in the cupholder I combed my hair as much as I could and put it into a makeshift bun. It was the best I could do, but at least it would keep my hair out of my eyes. I took one final look at myself and began the long walk towards the gates.

For two days I had walked the crowd, searching for familiar faces. I had prayed that I would turn a corner and hear that familiar, high-pitched squeal, and Trevor would come bounding into my arms. He would nearly knock me over like he does, and then Greg would come rushing behind him. He would sweep us both into his strong arms, and he'd tell me that it was all just a bad dream. If what my family had said in the alley was true then they were here, I just had to find them. Somewhere in the throngs of lookie-lous and zealots was my son, and if it was the last thing I did I would find him, alien-infested or not. I was getting him out of here, but I had to get to the gates first.

You could feel the energy at the gates the closer you got. The crowd changed around you, becoming more intense, more on edge. Instead of the thrum of music from the tents on the outskirts of the makeshift town you could hear voices yelling, chanting their slogans or orders over and over again.

"Get back! Everyone turn around and head back!" I heard a strong voice shout before the crowd of travelers surged towards me, almost knocking me over. A uniformed officer in riot gear stood in front of me. We were still at least a mile away from the gates, but I could clearly see the protesters surrounding it just up ahead. A line of officers, their bodies forming a makeshift barricade, tried to keep the ever-growing crowd from becoming a part of it.

I continued moving forward, ignoring the shouts around me. If I was going to find my family, that's where they'd be. An officer's hand went up as I tried to pass, her face heavy with exhaustion and covered in sweat. "Turn away from the gates ma'am," she said, her eyes pleading with me.

"I can't," I said, "My son is in there. I have to get him."

She looked me over a moment, face fraught with worry. She didn't want to be here any more than I did, but we both had a job to do. She nodded towards me, letting me through reluctantly, and turned back to the tide of people coming towards us. "Get back! Everyone turn away from the gates and turn back!"

I moved through the crowd, and it was so thick with anger that it was almost palpable. The scent of sweat and stale piss almost made me gag. By the looks of it the number of "Truth Bringers" had over-taken that of the "Protectors", thanks to the new surge of bus-brought visitors. The Protectors were now in line with the military, their backs facing the gates to make sure no one could get behind them. Those coming would physically have to go through them to get to the facility, and that wouldn't be easy.

The chanting of the crowd was much clearer now. "The truth is HERE!" I could see Carrie above the crowd at the front, standing on a picnic table facing the gates with a megaphone in hand.

Things were about to turn for the worse. I could feel it in my bones, a whisper of death on the wind. I needed to find Trevor *now*. I searched the crowd, desperately weaving my way through bodies. They were packed in like sardines, all marinating in their own juices of sweat and piss. I stepped over a few people that had fallen, either from heat stroke or because they had been pushed. I was careful not to trample them as the crowd surged like waves, back and forth towards the gate. A tide of bodies on the ocean, held back by one lady on a picnic table and a row of guns.

"TREVOR," I screamed. "TREVOR!"

All I could hear was the beat of my heart in my ears and the relentless chanting. I struggled to keep my breathing even, but there were so many people. I had barely slept from worry since Monday, it was hot, and I was dehydrated. I should have drunk that water this morning instead of putting it in my bag. I was so fucking hot. Darkness began to seep into the corners of my eyes.

Don't pass out. Don't pass out.

I began to feel dizzy, swooning onto the person beside me. Hands gripped my shoulders, keeping me upright before I could fall.

"Hey, are you alright?" a familiar voice asked.

"I am fine honey, just tired," I said automatically, my brain recognizing the voice but not processing the meaning of it. It was Greg's voice.

I snapped awake. "Greg?" I said as I wrapped my arms around him, placing my head on his chest and breathing in the scent of him. I felt his arms wrap around me for a moment, as if this thing understood I needed to pretend for just a moment that everything could be the same again. Once my head cleared and the dizziness passed I pulled away. His blue eyes stared back at me, but they didn't carry the same warmth, the same sparkle of lift at the corner they had when he used to see me. This wasn't Greg anymore.

My head now clear I looked around him, searching for Trevor in the crowd. I could see Ashley and the boys not far away, their hair a fire of red in the desert sun, and I wondered if these aliens knew they needed sunscreen. My parents were off to their far side, and I could see them still holding hands. *No, no. Not what I'm here for.*

"Where's Trevor?" I grabbed his shirt, noticing the "The truth is Here" logo for the first time. Everyone in my family was wearing one of those t-shirts. In fact, most of the crowd was wearing one of those shirts.

"Don't worry, he's safe," he said, trying to calm me by putting his hands on my shoulders.

"Don't fucking touch me. Where's my son!?"

"We left him in the camper. It is parked close to the highway right over there, past the camp." He pointed in the direction of the Truth Bringers camp. I had walked through one of the meetings the other night, hoping I would see one of my family members in the crowd, but they hadn't been there. It was all a little too hippy-dippy for me, so I had left right as they had started passing out bottles of something. The last thing I needed was to get involved with a cult that literally handed out an unmarked substance and called it Kool-Aid.

"Did you...Is he...?" I tried to get the words out, but I couldn't. A lump of pain and worry stuck in my throat as I tried to ask the question. Was Trevor one of *them*?

"He is intact, he is whole," Greg answered. His blue eyes went soft around the edges. "Think what you will of us, but we would never harm an undeveloped. I know you have questions, but we have no time. If you want to see your son again you must go, now. Things are happening, and I will not stop them for the sake of one human child."

The intensity of his voice scared me, and I had never heard that tone before from Greg. It was filled with power and determination, and just a hint of fear.

I looked over at my parents, my sister, and my nephews. I had a feeling I would never see them again. We'd never have another family weekend, and I'd never hear my mother's voice over my answering machine asking me how to fix 'the Facebook' again. Trevor would never get to listen to one of my Dad's tall tales or have another sleepover with his cousins where they spend all night telling scary stories. I stopped myself from rushing over to them, Greg's words of warning echoing in my mind.

I looked up at Greg, his soft blue eyes an exact match to Trevor's. My boy would never hug his father again. My eyes filled and I held back a sob. "I love you," I said to the body of my husband, embracing him one last time, his warmth familiar.

"He loved you too," it replied.

With that I turned towards the camper and started making my way through the crowd. It was hard forcing my way through because the crowd was surging towards the gate, but I pushed on. I stole one last glance back at Greg, who was now talking to someone else while huddled over over a backpack. He turned towards me, mouthing a single word.

"Run."

I needed no more incentive. Something was about to happen, and I didn't want to be there for it. I was beyond being polite as I shoved my way through the crowd, yelling and clawing until it began to thin. I ran past the barricade of police, through the Truth Bringers' camp, past the meeting place. Fire burned in my lungs as I frantically weaved through the parked campers and tents. I climbed on top of a picnic table, hoping to spot the camper, but it was no use. Row upon row of campers and tents had been set up, all the way to the highway two miles out. I would have to do this the old-fashioned way.

I ran straight towards the highway, just as Greg had directed me. I didn't want to trust him, but I had no choice. Hitting the road I chose a direction and ran, weaving in and out of the first few rows until I spotted it. It was just as I remembered it. It was one of the last campers in the village, on the side of the road almost two miles from the gate.

I scrambled up the stairs and tried the side door. Locked. Desperately I began knocking on the window, hoping that someone was in there.

"Trevor, baby, Mommy's here. Open the door for Mommy!" I cried, my eyes heavy with tears that I refused to shed. But no one was there. My body crumpled against the door, too exhausted and devastated to keep standing. He had lied to me. Trevor wasn't there.

"Mommy!"

A high pitch squeal exploded from the side of the camper, and I heard quick footsteps coming towards me. Trevor's body crashed into me, his arms wrapping around my neck so tightly that I couldn't breathe, but I didn't care. I engulfed him in my arms, holding him just as tight. I peppered him with kisses, and his soft blond hair smelt fresh and newly washed. His clothes were clean, and they even matched.

"Ew, Mommy, you smell," he said, pulling away from me and wrinkling his nose. I smiled at that, and grabbed him, hugging him close.

"I know Monster. Mommy has had a long couple of days, and she missed you very much." I was unable to control my tears now. "But we have to get going."

"Why are you crying Mommy? Where's Daddy? Don't tell Daddy I left the camper, but I wanted to use the pee bush again like we did last night when we got here! Adrien and Thomas showed me how to pee on a tree so no one can tell! Wanna see?" he asked, pointing to a large, dried-out bush just a few campers away. "Are Nana and Papa coming? They said they had to do something important, but that they would be right back."

I looked at him, his sweet smile so innocent and unaware. For whatever reason these aliens had kept Trevor in the dark as to what was going on, and about who they really were. He had no idea that they were really aliens, and for that I had to give them thanks.

"No Monster. Daddy, Nana and Papa aren't coming back home with us, but they love you very, very much." I said, reaching out to rub his shoulder. Trevor's brow furrowed in confusion. He looked so much like Greg. He didn't understand and I didn't have time to explain. "How about we go get some ice cream?"

"Yes! Can I get two scoops, chocolate and cookie dough? Please?" he said, pulling away from me and running to the passenger-side door and opening it. Of course *that* door was open.

"Yes Monster," I said and grabbed him, hugging him once more tightly.

"Mom ... can't breath," he giggled.

"Sorry honey," I said, looking back one last time towards the gates, and the family I knew I would never see again. " Let's go get that ice cream."

NEILA

12:30 P.M.

I hate this fucking heat.

My coat, which I refuse to take off because it's got three guns and a handful of knives concealed within it, is going to be the death of me. On the plus side I'm not the only person who smells rank, and maybe my stench will help me push through the crowd faster to get to the officers up front. The police here are laughable, and they keep failing as they struggle to form any sort of cohesive line, but I need to talk to them about what I heard. If only they would just beat everyone back with a couple of nail-studded bats then everything would be better, but *nooooooooo*, that's inhumane.

Damn aliens.

If we could just open-fire on the crowd of crazies

then that would fix half of what's wrong at these gates, but the law enforcement here isn't exactly good at looking for palms with holes in them. Even if they knew what I know they wouldn't be organized or efficient enough to weed out who here is a host, and who's just an innocent bystander. At least all of the roads have been shut down, and they've stopped bussing people in, so there should be at least a few less aliens who made it here.

I wouldn't even be trying to get to the gates if I hadn't followed the group of gloved people out of that disgusting bar last night. One of them had dropped a glove, which I had picked up, and along the inside were tiny dots of evenly-spaced, dried blood. That was a common indicator of the Tau race of aliens, so I unhesitatingly followed them back to their campsite. I lost sight of them last night, my drinks making me a bit slower than usual, but luck was with me today when I came back out to look for them.

I was rounding a corner when I heard a group of voices, ones that were trying too hard to be quiet. It was the same weirdos from the bar, and I could practically see my numbers on the office scoreboard going up. The group's harsh whispers were out of place compared to the crazy volume of the main crowd, and I found myself sneaking around to the far side of the camper that they were closest to. They were huddled in the barely-helpful shade of a ragged umbrella, and I strained to hear them.

I couldn't make out all of their words, but I could see the holes in the sweaty, red palm of the only person missing a glove.

"...bomb..."

"... get right up to the gates..."

"They wouldn't kill their own, but we..."

"...mass explosion!"

"We'll be far enough out of the way..."

"Carl..."

I had heard enough. Whatever they were planning wasn't going to go well for us humans, and I had to make my way to the gates to warn the guards. I wanted to shoot this bunch down, to plunge my knife into their host body's eye socket until the worms crawled out and shriveled up in the intense heat, but they were moving away from the umbrella. I didn't have time to chase them down, no matter how much my muscles screamed for me to run after them.

There was also the chance that I would be outnumbered, so unless I could get them one-on-one it wasn't worth it when there were more pressing matters. I would remember those faces though, and

Jerry's score could kiss my ass when I breezed past it with more kills than him this year. That bonus was going to be mine, and I would finally be able to help my grandpa restore his farm.

It took me fifteen minutes of shoving people out of my way to get to the gates, and I was pissed by the time the gun-toters were in my sight. Those fucking aliens, their minds clearly a few Corn Flakes short of a balanced breakfast, were going to kill a whole bunch of people for no apparent reason. What was wrong with them? If they wanted a war then this would be a damn good way to start one.

As I took yet another elbow to my ribs I was sorely regretting my decision.

For the first time in a decade I was in a crowd of people, and I wasn't trying to see everyone's palms. It was a weird sensation, almost like I wasn't me, but I guess it was the first time I had a more pressing goal than alien hunting. Normally I wouldn't let potentially infected people within touching distance, but there was no other way for me to get near the gate. My only paper-thin reassurance was that, by now, the aliens should have amassed whatever muscle power they needed, so they weren't likely trying to infect people in the crowd with so many potential observers.

That didn't stop me from keeping a twitchy-fingered hand near my closest knife, but it allowed me to focus more on my quest. I could finally see the militia a few rows in front of me, their badges blindingly reflective, and that was when something went wrong. Some of the officers began firing into the air and, like a herd of wildebeests being chased by hyenas, the crowd began stampeding. I saw a tidal wave of faces surge towards me, and I closed my eyes as I braced for impact. There was nowhere to run to with all of the bodies packed behind me, and there was nothing to take shelter behind.

The first person to smash into me was a tall man, and with my boot heels sinking into the sand he was just at the right height to ram his elbow into my eye. I latched onto his belt to keep my balance, and as I steadied myself I nearly pulled his shorts off. Another body was flung into his, and the three of us toppled over in a heap. The tall man let out a shriek as a boot slammed down onto the bridge of his nose, and I let out an eerily similar cry as feet began trampling my ribs and legs.

I couldn't breath.

Between dust, pressure, extreme heat and panic my lungs were failing me, and in a blind panic I used his body as leverage to stand up. I had a fleeting thought to help him and the other person up, but I was swept away in the moist press of bodies before I could reach my hand out. He was rapidly out of sight, and I almost thought I would make it out with relatively minor injuries.

That was when another set of gunshots rang out, and the already-screaming mob surged with renewed frenzy.

When I went down a second time I felt bones break as my arm and leg were used as stepping stones. I tried to fight the legs off, and to shout for help, but no one heard me over the ghoulish chorus of dozens of screams. A foot kicked me so hard that I saw black spots, and I could feel a trickle of blood coming from my ear as my vision went dark. The liquid was almost cooler than the air around me. Who would have thought that my own species would kill me?

The very people that I had come here to protect and save were about to overwhelm me, and there wasn't a fucking thing I could do about it.

CARRIE

I could feel the crowd behind me, their angry voices raising in sync with mine as we shouted towards the gates, and to the mass of Drones lined up before it. In the hours since sunrise the crowd behind me had morphed from a picket line of Truth Bringers into a mob, one that was thirsty for blood and answers. A mob can't really be ignored, and by the looks of the camera crews and the growing military presence behind the gate, it wasn't. *Finally.*

Our group now dwarfed that of the Drones, outnumbering them ten to one, but that didn't seem to faze them. They stood shoulder-to-shoulder at the ready, and like robots they all had the same posture, the same exact stance. I had gotten the impression more than once over the last few days that they were not your run-of-the-mill government nutballs, but more like a unit that had been paid to be here. They were triggermen for the government. If the cards were down, and hard decisions had to be made, then the government would be able to blame the bloodshed on the crowd, not their own men.

Behind them were what I expected to see of the Drones: men and women of all ages, adorned with red, white, and blue hats and mismatched camo. They weren't in a nice, organized line, but they added a bit of extra muscle. High-power assault rifles were strapped to their backs, or carried in front of them, and they muttered angrily to each other as they walked back and forth from the group to the small shade tent they had set up for reprieve from the heat. I could see their bodies weaving under the assault of the sun, and they looked exhausted and weary. They were sunburnt, sick and trigger-happy.

It was a deadly combination.

Months before I couldn't fathom why Craig had insisted on spending his hard-earned money on hiring a logo designer from California to put together the "The truth is HERE" logo. I was dumbfounded when he told us he was having hundreds of these t-shirts made just to hand out at the gates, and it seemed like such a waste of money at the time. It all made perfect sense now. These weren't just t-shirts, this was a uniform. *Our* uniform.

The night before, at the last Truth Bringers meeting, the energy in the group had changed. We were preparing for battle, and we all knew it. Craig and Heather had stocked the front line with bottles of water under the picnic table. It was going to be another hot one, and even with the umbrellas the heat of the day was overwhelming. I downed another bottle of water, the cool liquid soothing my parched throat. I had gotten used to the slight burn on my tongue, even looked forward to it. The burst of energy was immediate, and so was the slight euphoria it gave. Whatever vitamins they had put in the water I was a big fan of, and by the look of the crowd so were they.

It was time, and I could palpably feel it. The crowd pushed towards the line, inching closer, their frenzied voices filling the air. They were ready, they just needed someone to pull the metaphorical trigger. I grabbed my megaphone and turned towards the crowd behind me, facing the thousands of people who had gathered since daybreak. Each of their faces were contorted in rage as they faced towards the gate, and they shouted four simple words again and again.

"The truth is HERE!"

I waved my hand and a hush fell upon the crowd.

"When the Facebook event went viral all those months ago I knew that this was our chance. We just needed to get enough people here at the gates, and we all need to demand answers. And look, here we are! We are HERE!" I waved my hand towards the crowd as they erupted in cheers, linked together forever in that one moment. I could see a grouping of black umbrellas in the distance, huddled together at the edge of the group. *What's going on?*

I turned towards the gates and the huddled masses. The tanks and armoured vehicles that had been positioned further out were now making their way to us, kicking up a trail of dust in the distance. "People of Area 51, you government officials and military. Our request is simple: stop lying to your citizens about what's happening in Area 51! Tell us the truth, that's all we want, all we've ever wanted. We aren't going anywhere until we get it! We deserve the truth. We want the truth!"

I was looking behind me as the crowd roared, watching them raise their fists towards the sky, when I saw Craig. His arms were frantically waving in the air to get my attention as he pushed through the crowd towards me. He was drenched in sweat, his cheeks flush with excitement and heat. He looked moments away from heatstroke, but he kept struggling to reach me, his eyes fraught with worry. I stepped down from the picnic table, cutting my speech off before I could lead the charge, and stepped into the crowd below me. They automatically moved to give me space to walk through, and they began to pick up my chant.

"The truth is here! The truth is here!"

"Carrie," Craig exclaimed when he finally got to my side, "They aren't letting anyone else through. The police, they have set up a perimeter around us, and I heard a swat team was coming to break up the crowd. They even put up a roadblock to stop people from getting any closer to the gates. They say it is for safety reasons, but you know the truth."

I did know the truth. They knew we were close, and they were doing everything they could to stop us from breaking through the gates. They were going to break us up like we were a fucking peace rally.

I climbed back onto my picnic table, and in the distance I could see a line of black-clad men and women marching towards us. They were moments away from the outlying barrier that the police had set up over half a mile away, their large guns and shields at the ready.

One... two... three... four... five... six... seven... eight... nine... ten...

Craig pulled a backpack I hadn't seen before off his shoulder, thrusting it at me.

"We said we would do anything to get the government to finally admit what is going on here. Did you mean it?" His eyes searched mine, and he was deadly serious.

"Yes, you know that. After everything I've been through, that Patricia's been through, enough is enough. I can't stand it any longer, not after this week and not after being believed by so many people. I've been seen as a person of worth, with something important to say, and I want to protect that." My chest was heavy with emotion. Memories of years of being bullied and teased because of what happened to me came rushing back, and I winced at the onslaught of the pain. "I'm sick of being treated like less because of what happened to me. Sick of being the butt of every joke, of being called crazy. I'm not crazy, *this* is fucking crazy. They have guns pointed at us because all we want are answers!"

"All we want is the fucking truth," I screamed at

the line of drones. They were standing at the ready now, just waiting to pounce on us.

One... two... three... four... five... six... seven... eight... nine...ten...

"We knew when we started this that there might be casualties. They will never let us through unless someone forces that gate open." Craig gripped my hands for just a moment, his black gloves hot on my skin. He released my hands, then opened his bag and pulled out a cylinder. "You are our leader Carrie, you have to get us through those gates."

I nodded, grabbing the bag and clutching it to my chest. My head swam with the reality of what I was just about to do. I could see the military in front of me, gathering closer to the gate, positioning themselves as a show of strength for the oncoming police force. They knew it was over. There was no other way, and I had no choice.

I knew what I had to do, but I had to make a call first. Thankfully she picked up on the first ring.

"They aren't going to let us in," I croaked.

"What? Honey, I can hardly hear you. I'm watching the protest on Youtube. They're bringing in the SWAT team so you have to get out!"

"They think this is a fucking joke, Patricia. If we leave now we did all of this for nothing. It's going to change nothing, not unless we can break down the gates for good."

"What are you talking about, Carrie? What do you mean for good?"

"They won't be able to ignore this babe, I promise. They won't be able to sweep us under the rug anymore."

"What are you..."

"They won't be able to call us crazy anymore, not after everyone sees what's in there. I love you."

I began walking towards the gate, my cell in one hand the backpack clutched to my chest with the other. I could hear Pat yelling through the phone, but I wasn't paying attention. I was staring right at the gates, through the hordes of Drones and military before it. I just needed to get close enough.

"Stay back from the gates!" It was the same asshole from the other day, the one with Heather, but I ignored him as he shouted at me. He had moved to the front of the line, along with an official-looking military officer. The Dones drew their guns towards me. "Do not move any closer, or we will shoot."

I ignored them. I could hear shouts behind me, and I knew that the SWAT team was making their way closer. They were trying to disperse the crowd, but it was too late. A few had broken away and begun charging at the gate, yelling as gunshots rang out.

"Hold your fire, hold your fire," the officer shouted, but the damage had already been done. The crowd behind me stampeded in panic, running from the onslaught of bullets.

"I love you, Patricia, so much. You're my light in the darkness, and I'll never forget you. I'm doing this for you, for all of us."

Ignoring the chaos around me I grabbed the cylinder from the backpack, looking over its smooth body. I found the small button on the bottom with my index finger, and I was almost close enough.

Ten... nine... eight... seven... six... five... four... three... two...

GERALD

12:43 P.M.

The lab was spotless. It hadn't been this clean at any point during my tenure, because I had never spent four hours cleaning it before. The last evidence of the morning's carnage, besides the two corpses, was my lab coat. I was scrubbing it over the utility sink, but it was no use. I was exhausted from cleaning, and I couldn't scrub the blood out. It was impossible to hide against the bright white fabric, and in that moment it occurred to me that I had spent very little time thinking about how to get out of there. What was the best way? Run? Try to overtake a guard and steal a gun and shoot my way out? Just walk out as if nothing was wrong? None of them seemed like good options, but the last one seemed like the least bad option. Maybe if...just then a rustling sound came from the corner of the room.

Carl was awake.

In a snap judgment I abandoned the lab coat in the sink, caring more about rushing over to the gurney. I lifted the sheet just as Carl was raising his forearms, his eyes fluttering open as he took in his surroundings.

"Carl!"

He coughed and hacked.

"Carl, you okay? You hanging in there?"

"*COUGH...*yes. *COUGH COUGH.*"

"I'm right here buddy. Are you able to stand?"

"Gerald, you really did a job on this host...*COUGH.*"

"I know, I'm sorry. I'm not a surgeon. Is this going to work? Are you secure?"

He lifted his torso and spun his legs around so that they dangled off the edge of the gurney. "Yes. I think...this will work."

I hurried back over to the sink to collect my badge, and I told Carl the plan as I wiped the blood off of the outer plastic, "So I think our best chance is to just walk out of here. The guards know both of us. My lab coat is fucked, but..." Carl hadn't moved, and that disturbed me. I shot a look over my shoulder to check on him.

He was sitting there, in Magruder's body, with his arms rigid at his sides. His fists were pressing into the cushion of the gurney, and he had a look of sheer horror on his face.

I stopped what I was doing and made my way back over to him. "Carl? Carl, what's wrong?"

He shifted his eyes to meet mine, moving nothing else. "Gerald," his jaw trembled as his mouth tried to form words, "I...I can see his mind... Magruder, this place... what he has seen, has done to my kind..."

"Stop." I clamped both of my hands down on his shoulders. "Carl, I don't want to know. Don't tell me. Whatever it is, I don't want it. You take it, use it. Use it to get us out of here or to get you home, but leave me out of it. I need to try to put this behind me."

His eyes told me he understood, but his jaw told me he was still reeling in shock from whatever it was that Magruder had seen, had done, and had discovered. I had meant it when I said I didn't want to know. As I turned around to grab my badge I heard him whisper, "Gerald, it will never be behind you."

Luckily, getting out of S-4 was a lot easier than getting in. The plan was simple: walk through the three internal doors between the lab and the exit, walk out the front door, walk past the guards without saying a word, walk to the bus lot, wait for the next bus to Area 51, board a plane and then head to Vegas. With any luck maybe we could get a drink together at a real bar before we parted.

"Okay. You ready, Carl? Ready to go home?"

"Let's get outside the facility first, Gerald."

"Right." I opened the door to the hall that would lead us outside, and we both stepped through the doorway. I didn't look back as the door slammed behind us. I hadn't anticipated just how gratifying the sound would be.

As we strode together down the hall I felt a rush of confidence in the plan I had hatched, and it felt like this was going to work.

Some jackoff lab tech, whose name I didn't know, walked past us with a sneer, "Forget your lab coat, Gerald?"

I ignored him and kept walking. If only he knew.

We got through the next two doors without a hitch. As we turned down the final corridor, towards the exit, my heart began to pound at the sight of the two guards holding their massive machine guns. "I'll go first," I whispered to Carl.

I was sweating through my shirt so heavily that it must have looked like I was sick. "You alright, sir?" one of them asked.

"Just fine, a bit warm in there today, that's all." I said with the fakest smile you'd ever seen. I walked through the MAG and put one hand on the long, bar-handle of the door to the outside. I turned around to see Carl successfully pass behind me. I smiled for real this time and opened the door.

"Sir, excuse me!"

Fuck. What? We both turned around.

"Are you sure you're alright, sir?", the other guard took a hand off his gun and pointed to a single drop of blood on the white tile floor, the last tile before the threshold of the door. Without thinking, Carl put his hand to the back of his neck. Doing so squeezed three more drops of blood out of the hack-job neck wound. With his hand still on his neck, Carl turned around and said, "I'm fine. Just..."

Both guards now had their guns drawn. "Both of you, please, step back inside. Now."

Carl turned back to me, burning a hole through

me with his gaze, as if to say, 'What the Hell do we do now?'

We were already outside, though I still had my hand on the door to hold it open. I didn't know if the door was bulletproof, but I had to assume it was. I closed my eyes for a second, calmed myself, and shoved the door closed.

"RUN! Come on, it's not far!"

We heard shots ring off the inside of the door as we sprinted towards the bus lot, and our only hope now was that there was a bus already there. The guards opened the doors and started firing at us for real. Carl, considering he was in Magruder's body, was faster than I was. At this point he was more important than I was, so I drafted behind him in case a bullet strayed too close. Seconds later pain ripped through my left shoulder as a bullet passed through it. In an odd way it didn't hurt as much as I had always imagined it might. Don't get me wrong, it hurt like Hell, but it wasn't enough to slow me down for more than a heartbeat.

The one I took fifteen seconds later to the lower back was. "OHHH, FUCK!!" That one hurt. I put my hand to my back and slowed down, panting, gasping for air, ready to give up.

Carl stopped running, spun around, and made a beeline back to me. He grabbed my good shoulder, threw it over his, and ran for the both of us. "Thank you, Carl..." I whispered through the commotion.

The guards hadn't moved from the door, and the shots had stopped. It didn't mean we were in the clear at all, if anything it meant that the full force of Area 51 security was being roused from its slumber and was about to be rained down upon us.

Finally, the bus lot was in sight. There was a single bus sitting right in the middle of the lot, facing the exit. It was as if had been placed there by Carl himself. In fact, I started to wonder if he somehow had. It wouldn't be the weirdest thing I had seen in this place, not by a long shot.

We hobbled over to the bus door, and it opened. The driver started to greet us, but stopped as soon as he noticed the blood on me. "Get out, now!" Carl screamed at the driver. Without hesitating the driver grabbed his paper lunch bag and scurried down the steps, casting us a final, wide-eyed glance as he reached the pavement. Carl plopped me in a seat, then he glanced at the wheel. He quickly hopped down the steps, managing to catch the driver before the man got far.

"Keys!?"

"They're in there, in the cupholder! Shit, man!"

Out of nowhere we heard the sound of a massive explosion. It was somewhat distant, and was followed by a ground tremor. The three of us spun our heads around to look in the direction of the blast, which had come from Area 51's main gate.

"The Hell was that?" the driver looked at us frantically, but Carl ignored him. The windshield was the only window on the bus, and a huge, metal divider separated the front cab from the rest of the seats behind it. For the first time in fourteen years I was about to see what this road looked like.

As soon as the keys were in the ignition Carl started the bus, quickly speeding away.

For a moment a sense of calm washed over me. The events of the last few hours were exhausting, and finally I felt like we could relax for a brief moment. I looked down at myself to see if I had any more wounds. It hurt like Hell to move my neck and bend my torso, and then I saw why. I had indeed sustained a third shot, and this one had ripped right through my right side. I was losing a ton of blood, and my moment of relaxation slipped right into despair.

"Carl..."

I tried to use my shirt to plug the steady rivulet of blood coming from my mid-section, but it wasn't doing much.

"Gerald, how badly are you hurt?" He took a brief look at me, which answered his question. His eyes widened as he saw the trail of blood leading from my stomach back to the door, and he paled a shade or two.

"Ahh-OW!" I was trying to apply more pressure, but I was tired. My breathing was still heavy, and it wasn't slowing down like I needed to. "Carl, I think this is bad."

He didn't seem to know how to react to that statement. "What does that mean?"

I thought about his question, and something came over me in that moment. The pain seemed to dissipate from my side, and I felt a deep sense of comfort in my neck and in my shoulders. "It means... you're free, Carl." I turned and looked at him with a huge grin on my face. He looked back at me like I was insane, but my mind had never been clearer in my entire life. I took my left hand off the stomach wound and slapped it down on his right thigh with a splatter of blood. Then, as if I had been given laughing gas, I started howling. "You're FREE, Carl!

Hahahaha! You're FREE! It's over! Haha!" I couldn't contain myself.

Carl kept his eyes on the road towards Area 51, but I saw a smile sneak across his face. It melted when we rounded a corner and saw a huge plume of smoke rising from the main Area 51 facility. It must have been a result of the explosion we heard in the parking lot.

"Gerald. Do you know what this is all about?"

I looked Carl over in a moment of pride. His hands were clenched at 10 and 2, his torso hunched over the wheel, and for someone who had only read about driving human vehicles he was doing admirably. There was a dark stain on his jacket just below the armpit. I watched as a drop of blood trickle to the ground.

I sat back in my chair and grinned. "You're free... you're free..."

A calmness washed over me. Far off in the distance and all by itself, I saw what looked like a house I lived in long ago. As the bus got closer I could see the figure of a woman, her dress familiar, standing on the porch. *Mom?* It couldn't be, she had been dead ten years now. I caught the vision of a yellow blur darting from the house. It came into focus and I choked out a laugh. *Charlie!?* I knew that face anywhere. My old yellow lab was running towards me and smiling from ear to ear, tongue flapping in the wind. I had forgotten what happiness looked like. A flash of white light washed out everything in front of me.

I sat back in the chair and closed my eyes.

Y*ou know, I'm pretty sure that, for this hitching thing to work, there has to be somebody around to pick you up...*

I had no idea how long I'd been walking. I'd tried counting my steps for a while, but I'd given up after two hundred. Funny thing, if I'd had my phone it would have been doing that for me. Not that it mattered anyway, I wasn't sure how much longer I'd last in the heat. They'd find me lying in the sand, surrounded by vultures. A Randy buffet. *Mark this down, my last shirt design. A crowd of vultures sipping margaritas, eating a Jimmy Buffet.*

I kicked myself for sleeping through everything, but I suppose I shouldn't have been too surprised. After a few rounds of drinking I had gotten to talking with a group of app developers from Colorado who had just come in. We laughed, we sang, and the next thing I knew we were back at their camper having a grand old time. I'm not sure what they had in that stuff they passed around, but I don't remember much else from that night except for a rousing round of Bohemian Rhapsody.

Whatever it was, it must have been good. I actually woke up this morning and I didn't feel half bad. It was, however, well after noon. I was in one of their trailers, sprawled out on the floor. I stepped outside and realized the camp was very much empty. Everyone had already left! I slipped my shoes on and took off running toward the gates.

I stopped as a voice shouted at me. "Hey you! Stop!"

I turned to see a cop running toward me, waving a hand. Then I looked past him and saw the roadblock. There were a whole bunch of officers standing around a row of cinder blocks staring out at the freeway. I raised my hands to show they were empty. "What's going on?"

"We can't let you go out there, sir. Things have gone too far, and we're clearing everyone out. We thought we'd gotten everyone, but here you are. Please clear out."

I closed my eyes. "You gotta be kidding me! All this way and I can't even go join the fun? This is just great." I looked past him again at the rest of his buddies, and I couldn't keep the scowl from my face.

He sighed as he followed my gaze. "We've closed down the freeway for miles, but they stuck us here to make sure no one gets through. So please don't make this any more difficult than it has to be. Party's over, go home."

I opened my mouth to say something that would probably get me into trouble when a series of pops echoed across the sand. I looked at the cop before me, and I froze as I saw his hand drop to his hip without looking at it, as if on pure instinct. "Is that..."

I didn't get any further before the sky lit up. We both turned and watched silently as a mushroom of sand blossomed up and spread across the sky, blocking out the mountain behind it. A few seconds later a blast of hot air washed over us, throwing sand up into our faces. As it settled down I found myself whispering the only words I had left.

"Party's over."

In the next moment all Hell broke loose. The entire crew of officers started running for their cruisers and driving off. The one I had been speaking to stopped and turned around, yelling back at me,

"What the Hell are you doing just standing there? Get back! Get to safety!"

Then they were gone, and I found myself standing in the desert. Alone So I did the only thing I could think of. I turned and started walking down the road. I had a feeling that waiting for somebody to come back around to give me a lift would leave me disappointed.

So here I was, sweating through my tiny shirt as I walked to God-knows-where, waiting for somebody to come along and take me away, or to just sit down and die...

The rumble behind me took a few seconds to register. I turned around in disbelief, my cracked lips curving into a smile. A bus was driving up the road toward me, its windows all blacked out with the exception of the front cab. I began jumping up and down, waving my arms frantically. I almost cried with relief as the bus pulled over and stopped just ahead of me.

I stumbled up alongside it and glanced in the passenger window. The first thing that caught my eye was the glowing clock on the front console. Finally, I'd be able to see how many hours I'd spent wandering out here. The display read... 1:30? Huh.

My eye was snatched from that by the body

slumped in the seat next to the driver. I couldn't make out any features, but I could tell he was dead. I suddenly thought of another window I had leaned into recently, of all the things I had seen since leaving home. Then I shrugged. If I was going to die at the hands of a psycho bus driver, screw it.

The driver's door opened, and out stepped a thin man with even thinner glasses. He tottered for a moment, as if unsure of which direction he was going to go, then dropped into the sand.

I was about to thank him for stopping, but then I noticed the hole in his side. His shirt was damp with blood. He struggled to push himself up and groaned, eyes screwed shut.

I sat down next to him. "You look even worse than I do buddy."

He seemed to notice me for the first time. He glanced over at me briefly, then his head snapped around and his eyes grew wide. I looked around before realizing he was staring at me. "What? Did I grow an extra head?"

He blinked once, twice, then relaxed. "Oh, never mind. You just reminded me of... someone I knew, a long time ago." He stopped, and a smile crept across his face as he looked down at himself. "Hey, friend. I think you can help me out. I need to get out of here, quickly."

I stood up and wiped off my knees. "You and me both. Tell you what, toss me those keys and we'll get you somewhere we can fix you up. Where are you heading, anyway?"

He held out his hand. "I just want to go home."

Never taking my eyes from his, I reached down and grasped his palm in mine.

EPILOGUE

"The small town of Rachel, Nevada has been devastated by the explosion that rocked the Storm Area 51 Facebook event yesterday afternoon at approximately 1:03 p.m. Although there has been no official death count by the local coroner, the missing and unaccounted for number in the thousands. With another thousand injured in hospitals all over Nevada, and even some airlifted to surrounding states, the tragedy has sparked an outcry from citizens around the world.

"Five extremist groups have already claimed responsibility for the attack online. The White House, however, has only confirmed in its official statement that this was indeed an act of terrorism, stating there

*was not enough evidence to point to any specific
group at this time.*

*"The internet is abuzz with conspiracy theories
about what really happened, from a drug-infused
crowd to an alien invasion gone wrong."*

*"That's right Diana. Video evidence from the
scene shows..."*

A strong tap on my shoulder pulled my attention
away from the flat screen mounted above the bar.
Images and videos captured from the event flashed
on half of the screen, one after the other, beside the
news anchors.

"Sir, the car is ready. We should leave now." I
looked up at the large host with blond hair standing
beside me. His brow furrowed over his light blue
eyes as he watched me take another sip of the foamy
liquid of fermented grains and hops that they called
beer.

"So awful. I can't imagine what type of person
would do something so evil," the bartender said
under her breath. She hadn't taken notice of me or
the man that had entered minutes ago since giving
me the beer, her eyes trained on the television and
the ongoing news report.

I grunted in response. I had seen enough over the
last seventy years to know that no human was inno-

cent, and evil came in many forms on this planet. I finished the drink in one gulp. Although I had remembered to grab Magruder's cell phone after exchanging bodies with the shorter man in the strange t-shirt, I had completely forgotten to collect his wallet. That left me with a total of two dollars and thirteen cents. Thank goodness the group of host's had found me when they did. I wasn't looking forward to explaining why I couldn't pay my bill, not that the bartender would have noticed. She was focused on the television, like almost every other person in the bar. I hopped off the tall barstool, making my way to the door and leaving the host with the bill.

Another host was waiting at the door for me, this one much younger, his bright red hair standing out in the dim lighting of the bar. He opened the door before I could reach for the handle, his hand riddled with red dots. It had been so long since I had the familiarity of a clan with me within a singular host. Since my imprisonment they had made sure to sepa-rate us, isolating us from one another in separate hosts or glass cages in the lab. I longed for the comfort of community, the sense of unity with the others, but found myself pulling away. It had been too long, and I had been through so much trauma the last few days from jumping from host to host. I needed to recuperate before I could add other Tau to this body.

"It is a good thing we found you when we did, sir. We were able to break into the facility after the explosion, but found no clan members within it. We had lost all hope that you had survived," he said as he opened the truck door for me, his voice hushed. I hoisted myself into the cab. This host body, although healthy and young, seemed smaller and more awkward than the majority of the hosts that had housed me over the last seventy years.

"I may have been in a cage for seven decades, but I still remember how to send out a simple frequency alert with coordinates," I said, tossing Magruder's cell phone in the cab beside us. "I am just amazed that these humans had all these years with our technology, yet they never noticed our transmissions. Not one. Fucking idiots."

"Sir, your original message in 1947 when the ship first split and crashed, noted over six hundred clan members were alive. What happened to..."

"There is no one left, I am the last of my clan," this body's voice croaked, a lump forming and making it impossible to continue. I cleared my throat. "Is the ship ready?"

"Yes sir, everything is ready. We were just waiting to collect the rest of...you. We were just waiting for you. We should be there in less than two days."

"Good, we need to get back as soon as possible, we have been away too long."

"Hopefully we are not too late. Do you think any other scouting missions were successful?"

"I do not know, but the faster we leave the better. We need to tell them the good news. We have found a planet that has the mineral resources we require in abundance." I looked out of the window, the hot sun glinting off the sign as we passed by it. *'Thanks for visiting Davenport, hope to see you soon.'* I smiled. "And more host bodies than we could ever have the need for. How fortuitous our crash landing was."

ABOUT THE AUTHORS

(signature)

MICHELLE RIVER

(ELAIN, CARRIE, EPILOGUE)

Michelle has always had a creative spirit and has a passion for painting, photography, pottery and writing. Michelle hails from Ontario, Canada where she lives with her wonderful husband and fearless daughter. A lover of hot black coffee and everything dark and terrifying, she spends her nights writing horror and dreaming about all the things that go bump in the night.

For fun she writes short horror stories on Reddit under the user name Drywitdrywine, and you can also follow her on Facebook.

This has been an amazing project to be a part of. I would like to thank the whole team of writers, their idea's and positivity throughout the process from conception to late night writing sessions were invaluable.

A big thank you to the people behind the scenes. Michele Freeman, for amazing advice and formatting *the book, my family, Elizabeth who did last minute edit suggestions, all the beta readers who took time to read and suggest, and my husband Scott, who tirelessly listened to me go on about worms and aliens. You are the best.*

ALANNA ROBERTSON-WEBB

(NEILA)

Alanna Robertson-Webb, known on Reddit as MythologyLovesHorror, is a medical Wound VAC specialist by day and a writer/editor by night. She lives in NY with a fiance and two cats, all of whom take up most of the bed space.

Alanna has been writing since she was five years old, and writing well since she was seventeen years old. Besides the written word she loves L.A.R.P.ing, swimming and playing board games.

Her short horror stories have been published in anthologies (such as *The Trees Have Eyes* by Haunted House Publishing and *Sirens at Midnight* by NBH Publishing), and she is forever on the lookout for inspirational material. Who knows, maybe YOU could be her next muse!

Thank you to everyone who supported me during this project. You know who you all are, and I love each of you.

BEN HARE

(RANDY, LOGAN)

Ben lives in Oregon with his lovely wife, two precocious kids, and a pair of cats who tolerate his existence. When he's not writing, Ben spends his days coding, acting, and making a general fool of himself. Ben has yet to meet any aliens, but Sasquatch does come to tea on occasion.

Thank you to my family for all the cuddles and support, especially the girl of my dreams for putting up with all the late nights and ridiculous conversations. Thank you to our beta readers for your invaluable feedback. And a big thank you to Carl... please don't enslave me!

DREW STARLING
(GERALD)

Drew Starling Gerald is a PR consultant who moonlights as a writer of horror and dark fiction. He lives in the Mid Atlantic with his wife and their poodle.

Thanks to Mulder, Scully, the guy from Millennium, Kubrick, Clarke, the "Aliens!" guy from History Channel and everyone out there who wants to believe.

ZANE HENSAL

(NATE)

Zane Hensal is a young horror author from Pennsylvania taking the world by storm. While managing day to day life as a teenager, he manages to scare us all with his supernaturally suspenseful horror stories. Zane found Internet popularity on the popular Reddit platform Nosleep under the username SMILEY_ATTACK.

Zane would like to thank his parents for the continued support throughout this whole process. As well as the creative team, and project manager, for giving him the opportunity to work on such an amazing piece!

Made in the USA
Columbia, SC
19 December 2019